MYSTERY BABYLON SERIES

BOOK 5:
THE GAZELLE

JAMIE LEE GREY

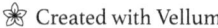

CONTENTS

1

A s the early morning sun broke through Alaska's cloudy skies, Austin Martin reached the end of the row of carrots and set down his weed rake. He stretched his back, then made his way through the forest behind the garden. A narrow deer trail led out to a rock outcropping overlooking the Inside Passage.

Deep blue water sparkled as waves danced in the salty brine. Austin scanned the water and the nearest islands for any sign of trouble.

More than a month had passed since the incident with the Coast Guard pirates, but the residents on Patmosa Island weren't ready to let their guard down. They'd established a round-the-clock guard station near the cove and marina, which was the most likely access point to the island.

A few other locations were accessible, as well, including Austin's tiny beach on the far side of the island – but it would take a seriously intrepid intruder to attempt to breach the Hideaway community from such a remote location. They'd have a long hike through a dense forest littered with downed trees, thanks to the mega-tsunami.

The little radio on his hip squawked.

"Pastor Austin?" Daisy Hemburg's voice came through the speaker as he pulled it from its holster. "Do you read?"

He winced slightly. Being called "pastor" was not something he would have chosen for himself, and he was a long way from getting accustomed to the term.

He pressed the button to talk. "I'm here. What's up?"

"We need you to come to the communications shack ASAP."

"Alright." He turned his back on the vast waterway and headed toward the forest.

"What's your ETA?" Daisy asked.

"Probably ten minutes." Austin strode through the trees, ducking wet branches that reached for his face.

"Hurry."

He didn't like the sound of that. "Roger that. Out."

Austin broke into a jog, soon reaching his garden, then hurrying past his single-room home and out to the main road. He glanced toward the Foresters' place across the road before hanging a right and heading toward Fellowship Farm.

Five minutes later, his heart rate was up as he entered the farm's gate. The communications shack was a tiny building on a hill behind the dairy barn. One of the local families operated ham radio equipment there, which had provided significant information to the island community in the past few months since the war. Windmills and solar panels generated electricity to power the gear.

A small crowd had gathered near the shack, but they made way for him to enter.

Sierra Forester stood just inside the doorway, and she gave him a glowing smile. He acknowledged her with a tilt of his head and a strained smile of his own. If she was happy, the news must be good, rather than the bad he'd expected on his run up here.

Decked out in a red, white and blue tie-dye t-shirt, Daisy stood beside the ham radio operator. She grinned at Austin.

"We got news from your family, Dustin!"

She would probably always call him that, and today he'd ignore it.

"My dad?" He stepped toward the radio apparatus. His father was in Bolivia, and he had not heard from him since the war.

"No. Your cousins and your grandfather!" Daisy beamed.

He stared at her, then turned to Sierra, who nodded and took a step toward him.

Austin could barely comprehend this. His grandfather had been in New York City until the war began, and his cousins had been attempting to get him out of his care facility, but they'd been snarled in terrible traffic. That was the last he'd heard from them.

Not long after that, NYC was nuked, and Austin had almost given up hope. He'd prayed for a miraculous escape for them, but over time his prayers had dwindled. It had been two months with no word.

Of course, communication these days was not like it had been before the war. Power was down almost everywhere in the United States, so phones and internet were not available. No texts, no email, no postal deliveries... for most of America, things were basically down to ham radio or smoke signals.

"Can I... can I talk to them?"

"They have limited electricity, so they said they'd check in." Daisy glanced at the clock on the wall. "In about five minutes."

"What did they say?" Austin glanced from her to Alfred

Herrington, the radio operator. "Where are they? Are they okay?"

"They're somewhere in Alberta, Canada. Making their way west to B.C." The old man eyed him. "They want to come here."

"Alberta?" He gawked. That was a long way from New York.

The mayor cocked his head. "They can't come here."

"What?" Austin bristled. "Why not?"

SIERRA FORESTER PURSED her lips as she eyed Mayor Jake Williams. Who did he think he was to prevent anyone from coming to Patmosa Island? He didn't own the place.

Besides, he had been the first to welcome the Coast Guard pirates last month. Now he thought he'd prohibit Austin's displaced relatives from seeking shelter here?

The gall of that man!

The mayor smoothed his grey hair and focused his steely blue eyes on Austin.

"We can barely feed ourselves." He patted his greatly-reduced stomach. "How on earth are we going to feed more people?"

"We're all growing gardens," Austin pointed out. "Hopefully, we'll be putting up a lot of produce this fall. They can help with the work."

Sierra considered adding her own input, but decided to remain quiet and watch how this played out.

"Hope is not a plan," the mayor countered. "Some of our crops may fail. Even if they don't, there's not enough food for us for the coming winter. Bringing in more mouths to feed is a terrible idea. It's bad for us, and it'll be bad for them, too. It's not like they'll be able to hitch a ride to the next community when we run out of food."

Sierra frowned. The man had a point. She didn't like it, and she really didn't like it applied to Austin, but maybe the mayor was right.

"They're my family," Austin argued. "If it was your family, you'd welcome them."

Touche! Sierra suppressed her smile.

The mayor never seemed to realize what a hypocrite he was – he was constantly applying one set of rules to himself and another set of rules to everyone else – but Austin had just nailed it.

"My kids were raised here," Mayor Williams answered. "They're already part of the community. Everyone knows them. This was their home. Anyone should be able to return to their home in a crisis."

He tilted his head. "Where are these cousins of yours from?"

Austin squared his shoulders and crossed his arms. "New York. Obviously they can't go back there."

"Well, now they're in Alberta, apparently. They should stay there. Canada wasn't bombed. Alberta is inland from the tsunami damage. Maybe they could settle in Calgary and make a new life for themselves."

Sierra's gaze slid to Austin. The mayor had made a reasonable suggestion.

Would he go along with it?

IN TOLBOLSK, Major General Ivan Orlov prepared for his first day back at work. Over the past month, he had persevered through tedious and sometimes agonizing physical rehabilitation. He was able to stand and walk now, although he still relied on a walker.

Before leaving the apartment, he paused in front of the mirror near the door. His skin looked pale, almost ashen, and deep wrinkles creased the corners of his tired blue eyes. He'd had a haircut yesterday in anticipation of his return to work, and now his brown hair was as tightly cropped as ever.

A piece of lint rested on the right shoulder of his uniform.

Marina noted it, too, brushed it off, and gave him a quick kiss. "Have a good day, my love."

"Thank you." He made his way awkwardly through the door she held open for him.

A black sedan idled at the curb, and the driver exited as Ivan approached. The man opened the passenger door for him, then took his walker and placed it in the trunk.

Moments later, they pulled into traffic and headed toward the Siberian kremlin.

Ivan released a sigh. The kremlin in Tolbolsk was a faint shadow of Moscow's magnificent kremlin, whose ancient towers and cathedrals had been nuked into oblivion by the Americans. How he hated those people!

Many Americans had died in the war and the days afterward, and now they continued to drop like the flies they were, succumbing to starvation and radiation sickness and old diseases like cholera and dysentery.

Still, some lived, and he hated the survivors. Foolish, ill-mannered and immoral, they deserved to die – and the sooner, the better. Who hadn't seen the internet videos of Kensington Avenue in Philadelphia? Or the footage of so-called peaceful protesters burning down American cities and murdering citizens and policemen? Or the sexual degenerates? They depicted the depravity of the general population.

Those people were worse than animals. At least actual

animals lived in a generally predictable manner and followed the laws of nature.

Americans, on the other hand, didn't know their right hand from their left. They could not tell their men from their women. They were fully insane, and the world would be a better place when they were eradicated from the earth.

Sodom and Gomorrah had nothing on them!

He was barely familiar with the tale about Sodom, but Marina had come home from the cathedral on Sunday talking about that old legend. She continued to pursue her newfound religious interest, and Ivan didn't object too loudly, because she had embraced sobriety at the same time. Perhaps it wouldn't hurt the children to attend church services for a while, and it certainly didn't hurt them to have a mother who was avoiding the vodka bottle.

Ivan's driver turned a corner, and the kremlin complex came into view. Located on a high bench overlooking the city and river, its majestic white stone walls and towers practically glistened. The ancient golden domes of the Sophia-Assumption Cathedral glowed in the early morning sun, perfectly accented by smaller domes of deep blue.

He had to admit they were beautiful. But nothing like Moscow.

The Russians had founded Tobolsk in the 16th century to serve as the center for developing Siberia. But the region was far-flung and inhospitable, and when the eventual Trans-Siberia Railroad did not approach the vicinity of Tobolsk, the city had fallen into obscurity for many decades.

Despite that, it remained the sole city in Siberia hosting a kremlin.

Only recently had Tobolsk pulled itself together as a new center for petrochemical production, utilizing liquids from the West Siberian oilfields.

Fortunately for Ivan and his military and government colleagues, Tobolsk had just opened a modern airport, as well. The small city of barely 100,000 residents had represented such an insignificant target, the Americans had not bothered to nuke it. Or if they'd targeted it, that missile had failed to reach its destination.

His driver slowed as they approached the kremlin, then he parked the car near an entrance and brought Ivan his walker.

A junior officer approached and saluted. "Good morning, Major General. May I show you to your office?"

"Please." Ivan shuffled into the building, passed through a security station, and followed the young man down a hall until he stopped beside a tall, polished door. The junior officer opened the door and stood aside as Ivan entered and made his way to his new desk.

His window looked out on the kremlin's observation deck, which boasted an array of antique artillery – and he had a nice view of the Irtysh River, as well.

He eased into his chair. An aide had left a red file folder on his desk, with a note reminding him of a meeting with the federation president and the military leaders which was set to commence in thirty minutes. Due to the modern threat of electronic hacking, Russia and other countries had returned to using physical paper for very sensitive documents – in some cases, even utilizing typewriters rather than internet-connected computers.

Ivan glanced toward the junior officer, who waited silently by the door. "Where is this morning's meeting to be held?"

The man snapped to attention but did not look Ivan in the eye. "In the conference room, sir. It's forty meters down the hall, on the left."

"Very well. You are excused."

The young man gave a stiff salute and exited, closing the

door quietly behind him.

Ivan's gaze drifted around his new office, taking in the gleaming windows, polished furniture and classic artwork. Two of the pieces he recognized as paintings by Ivan Shishkin, and a third, somewhat disturbing piece might have been Sergei Ivanov's – but he wasn't certain. They were likely replicas, anyway, since all of Russia's most valuable art had been cached in deep bunkers prior to the commencement of the war.

He turned his attention to the folder before him. He had previously read most of these briefs at home over the past week, but he noted some new details in the first pages of the memoranda.

The country's political leaders had presented a serious matter to the military for discussion and consultation. While Russia's major cities had suffered significant blows in the short nuclear war, much of its military remained intact, and the national leaders wished to seize the opportunity presented by the fall of their former nemesis.

America's destruction had presented a great void of power throughout the world, which was now reeling and destabilized.

Russia faced amazing opportunities at this time. For a brief period, she might be able to exert her military power in any number of directions as smaller, less militarized countries sought stability and strong allies.

Over the past two months, the political leaders had narrowed their focus on two options – seizing control of Israel and the Middle East, with its untold wealth of oil and trade routes, or reclaiming Russia's former territory on the North American continent. Alaska was now ripe for the taking, and it offered incredible natural resources, as well as a strategic foothold in the Americas.

Ivan glanced at the clock. He'd prefer to be early to this meeting. He tucked the folder under his arm and reached for his walker.

His mind was made up on the matter, and he'd do his best to sway his colleagues and the national leadership to his point of view.

Russia should move immediately to secure their former territory. Retaking Alaska would be a simple matter, and the only resistance would be offered by weak and starving locals. Sure, they all had handguns and hunting rifles, but they'd soon be out of ammunition and they were already out of food.

If an army marches on its stomach, Alaska's would keel over from hunger within a week or two.

IN HIS STUDIO apartment in Tel Aviv, Mao Wu Ying bent down to tie his shoelaces. The tiny room smelled faintly of sea air and fresh tahini cookies from the bakery across the street. His stomach growled, emphasizing his need for breakfast.

A sharp rap sounded on his door.

Wu Ying froze.

He was not expecting any visitors. Wei Min and Christian should be in their Hebrew language class at this hour.

Another knock, more insistent this time.

He moved cautiously toward the door, then stood on his toes to look out the peep hole.

A young Chinese man stood in the hall.

Wu Ying pulled away from the door. He did not recognize the man, and it was rare to see other Asians in this neighborhood – or anywhere in Israel these days. What could he want with Wu Ying?

Was that man a Chinese agent?

Did China intend to arrest Wu Ying and bring him back to stand trial for going AWOL from the People's Liberation Army? He had been in Israel for a month now, and in that time, the Chinese government had begun to pull itself together.

Power abhors a vacuum, especially in communist countries.

The stranger pounded on the door.

"Police! Open this door, or we will forcibly enter!"

Wu Ying gulped, then scanned the room for anything that could be used to defend himself from an attacker. He did not believe the first statement, but he did believe the second. That man was not a police officer, but he seemed determined enough to break in.

A heavy lamp stood on his bedside table, or he could grab a kitchen knife.

He reached for the knife, hid it behind his back, then opened the lock with his left hand.

Yanking the door open, he glared at the man. At the same moment, he noticed two uniformed Israeli police officers standing off to the side. They had not been visible through his peep hole.

"What do you want?"

"Mao Wu Ying. You must come with us." The man spoke Chinese, but with a strange accent.

"Why?"

"We will discuss that at the station." The man peered around him. "Is there anyone else in this apartment?"

"No."

"Are you armed?"

"A kitchen knife," Wu Ying admitted. No use hiding it from regular police. "In my right hand."

The Chinese man stepped back, and the police officers drew their weapons.

"Set it down on the counter," one of the officers ordered. "Slowly!"

Wu Ying did as he was told, taking a step toward the kitchen area and setting the knife on the countertop.

"Put your hands in the air, and step away from it!"

Wu Ying obeyed, and as he did, both officers rushed him. A second later, his hands were behind his back, and cold metal cuffs snaked around his wrists.

"What is this about?"

No one gave him an answer. They pulled him out of his apartment, guided him down the hall, and led him to a squad car. There, he was unceremoniously ushered into the back seat. The two officers got into the front, while the Chinese man entered a black sedan and pulled away from the curb.

The police car followed the sedan through Tel Aviv's clean, modern streets, finally pulling into the parking lot of a large government building. They rolled up to a side door, then stopped.

The building had few markings, and Wu Ying had not learned enough Hebrew to read them – but this place did not look like a jail. At least, not like the one where he'd been detained in Beijing. This looked more like an office building, with many windows and no razor wire.

Ahead of them, the Chinese man parked his sedan and entered the building. The police officers opened Wu Ying's door and helped him out. They accompanied him to the entrance.

Wu Ying's heart sank as he stepped though the doorway.

He sensed his life was about to change in ways he would not like, and could not evade.

2

R elying on the walker more than he'd like, Ivan shuffled into the kremlin's conference room. A massive rectangular table ran most of the length of the room, while additional chairs for aides or guests lined the walls on both sides and the back. At the front of the room, the great seal of the Russian Federation adorned the wall and was flanked by the national flag.

Red carpet emblazoned with gold filigree muffled his footsteps and the noise of his walker's wheels as he entered. There were no windows, but antique chandeliers provided plenty of light.

Arriving early for this meeting had been a good plan. Other than building staff setting up tea service, he was the first person to arrive. He'd be able to take his place without everyone watching his awkward entrance.

Ivan spotted his nameplate at the end of the table farthest from the president's seat. That seemed odd. Normally, he'd be seated near the president.

Was he still under a cloud from that issue with President

Abramov's granddaughter? His family had been cleared of any criminal wrongdoing in her tragic death.

Still, this seating arrangement spoke volumes to him. It had been done on purpose; he was certain of that.

He set his red folder on the table, pulled out the chair, and eased into it. Then he positioned the walker at the corner of the table where he hoped it would be unobtrusive.

Voices echoed in the hall, and he turned to see Major General Nikita Pavlov entering with Colonel Lev Balakin. The old general's watery blue eyes lit up as they focused on Ivan. His thick white hair seemed thinner today, and his face less flushed.

Pavlov stepped slowly toward Ivan. "Major General Orlov, it is good to see you again."

Ivan struggled to his feet. "And you as well, my friend."

"Please, don't get up on my account." The old man gestured toward Ivan's chair. "Rest yourself."

"I'm fine." Remaining standing, Ivan turned his attention to Colonel Balakin, one of his own Ground Forces subordinates. "I read the memoranda you provided. Do you have any additional updates?"

"Not at this time, sir."

"You did not indicate a preference for the options under consideration today," Ivan pointed out. "Alaska? Israel?"

The colonel averted his gaze for a moment, then met Ivan's eyes. "Obviously, Alaska has the more certain outcome and would be easier to seize. However, successfully subduing Israel could be Russia's crowning glory."

"I see." Ivan released a slow breath. "Thank you for your input."

The man gave a slight nod as Ivan turned back to Major General Pavlov. "Are you willing to share your thoughts on the matter before the meeting gets underway?"

"Your colonel gave a solid perspective," the older man answered.

Clearly, Pavlov did not wish to reveal too much, too early. He was a wise old bird. There was a reason he had politically survived so many decades of Russian intrigue and collusion.

Moments later, more military and political leaders began filing into the conference room. Several greeted Ivan, but he noted their words were not especially warm after his extended absence. No doubt that was due to the tarnishing of his reputation since the death of the president's granddaughter. He hoped to be able to work his way back into their good graces.

As the men began taking their seats around the table, it occurred to him that today would be a test for him personally. He would need to pass it, with flying colors, or expect to be quietly shuffled off to an early retirement or a civilian job.

The question was, what did he need to do to pass that test?

The answer came to him in an instant. He'd need to endorse whatever he perceived the president wished to do in this matter – regardless of his own military knowledge and understanding.

AUSTIN SHIFTED his focus from the mayor to Sierra. A look of consternation flickered across her face. She lowered her gaze to the floor, avoiding his eye contact. It appeared she agreed with the mayor's point.

And the man did have a point, but that didn't mean he was right.

Sure, resources here were limited, and Austin's family wasn't from this area – but did that mean the islanders should turn them away?

Austin focused on Mayor Williams.

"So you think we should turn away anyone who wants to come here, unless they were raised here?"

"That's a good place to start, I think," the mayor said.

Daisy tossed her long brown curls over her shoulder. "Now that's just silly. You weren't raised here, Jake."

"But I've been here for thirty years. I raised my family here." He gave her a withering look. "I'm the mayor, for crying out loud!"

Austin rubbed his chin. "It seems like you're trying to frame new rules that benefit you and your family."

"No, I'm trying to make sure there's enough food to go around this winter. And bringing in new folks is going to strain our very limited supply."

The radio squawked, and the ham operator responded. A moment later, Austin recognized his cousin Rick's voice.

"You there, Austin?"

Alfred, the ham, motioned him forward. Austin keyed the microphone. "I'm here, Rick. You got Grandpa out of New York?"

"Yes. He's with us. Sherry's here, and Louis."

"That's great! What about Maya?"

There was a long pause, and Rick's voice faltered a little when he answered. "We haven't been able to contact her."

Austin wasn't terribly surprised by that news. Maya was Louis and Rick's sister, and she'd been working in a U.S. intelligence agency in a suburb of Washington, D.C. when the war broke out.

"I'm sorry to hear that."

"Thanks." Rick inhaled noisily. "I need to keep this short, but wanted to reach you and let you know we're headed your way. I guess your place survived the tsunami?"

"I don't think so. The islands were devastated. I'm living in a little shack that used to be a woodshop."

"Oh." A long silence followed. "But you're doing okay, right? Hunting and fishing, maybe working on that farm there?"

The mayor glared at Austin as he leaned toward the mic to answer. "We're surviving. But we haven't had any resupply of food or fuel or anything."

"You've gone back to the pioneer days."

Austin choked a little at that description. "Without the necessary skills, tools, knowledge or experience."

"But with a radio and some kind of power source."

"Wind and solar."

"Huh." Another long pause. "Well, we're headed toward you. Should be to the coast soon. We're exchanging our valuables at pawn shops, getting Canadian currency. American money and credit cards don't work anymore. Anyhow, we hope to drive to Stewart or Prince Rupert."

Austin frowned. "And then how will you get here?"

"Could you come pick us up?"

He blinked. "That's a real long way, Rick. We don't have extra fuel for the boats. And the port facilities there on British Columbia's coast are almost certainly destroyed."

"Both communities have repaired at least one dock," his cousin responded. "So you can bring a boat in."

"If we can get fuel," Austin reiterated.

The mayor cleared his throat. He glared at Austin. "We don't have fuel for that!"

Austin ignored him. "Look, Rick... you guys might be better off staying there in Canada. That region in Alberta wasn't impacted by the tsunami or the nukes."

"Canada won't let us stay," his cousin countered.

"What do you mean, they won't let you? You're already there."

"Along with about a million other U.S. citizens who bailed into Canada, and now we have thirty days to get out."

Austin hesitated, then suggested, "I imagine you can blend in with the local population."

"That's not the problem. The government recorded our cell phone numbers as we crossed the border, and we're required to keep the phones with us at all times, and they constantly track our location and movement. When Americans ditch their cell phones, they hunt us down like criminals. Happened to a guy I met. They cuffed him and took him to jail."

Rick sighed before he continued. "Look, we have to return to the states, and Alaska is the only viable one. Grandpa's too old to run around like a convict, hiding from Canadian police."

"I understand."

"Hey, we need to cut this broadcast short. We're traveling west, and we'll find another ham operator along the way, so we can check in again."

"Okay. You've got the call sign for our guy here. I'll make a point of being near the radio each day at 7 a.m. and 7 p.m. Alaska time until I hear from you."

"Got it. We'll be in touch."

SIERRA BIT the inside of her lip as the radio transmission ended. Was Austin's cousin right? Had a million Americans fled into Canada at the outbreak of the war?

It was quite possible. Also, it was likely that many U.S. citizens and other residents bolted to Mexico, too.

If she'd been living Outside, in the Lower 48, when the war broke out, she'd probably have headed for a neighboring country if she could. Nobody wanted to be killed in a war at home.

She glanced from Austin to the mayor, who was staring at him.

Austin crossed his arms and leaned back against a black metal filing cabinet.

The mayor jammed his thumbs into his belt loops. "We can't feed extra people."

"You mentioned that already." Austin eyed him. "And you heard what my cousin said. A million Americans are going to be expelled from Canada in the next few weeks."

"Where are they gonna go?" Mayor Williams widened his eyes. "They can't come to Alaska! That's more than our state's highest population, ever!"

Sierra wasn't sure if that was true, but she knew in her lifetime, it was. Alaska had fewer than 750,000 residents spread around a gigantic land mass.

Now, many of them were dead or starving.

What would happen if a million more arrived, bringing nothing with them but their suitcases and their hunger?

Daisy tugged on the hem of her tie-dyed shirt. "See this red, white and blue? We're all Americans here. We'll pull together. We'll help each other out. That's what we do."

Sierra hoped her friend was right. But she feared Daisy's perpetual optimism might not pan out this time.

A million refugees was a shocking number. Especially for a war-torn, tsunami-battered little island chain in a cold, wet, inhospitable landscape.

Most of these people, like Austin's relatives, would have no skills to live here. They wouldn't know how to hunt, how to be safe around bears, how to cut down a tree without dropping it on their head, how to fish, or anything useful.

Maybe they wouldn't make it to Patmosa Island. Hideaway

was a long way from the two northern ports accessible via road in British Columbia. Surely no one would attempt to reach Alaska from B.C.'s southern ports – it was such a long trip. Thirty boat hours, at least, from Vancouver to Ketchikan, and perhaps another thirty to Hideaway. Well, on the slow ferry, anyway. Other boats traveled *much* faster.

Mayor Williams frowned at Daisy.

"It's going to take a lot more than a little rah-rah helping each other out. Even now, our local group is barely able to feed itself. And we've got a farm, a cannery and smokehouse and a couple of functional boats. These people are bringing nothing to the table. Literally."

Daisy planted her hands on her hips. "How do you know what they're bringing? They might have skills. There might be doctors, mechanics, and construction workers coming."

He shook his head. "Doesn't matter, though, does it? Unless they're bringing boatloads of medical supplies, tools, spare parts and equipment with them. And you know they're not."

Sierra exhaled a quiet sigh. She glanced at Austin.

A sad, faint smile turned his lips as his gaze met hers. He shrugged and gave her an almost imperceptible wink.

She tried to send him a brave smile in return, but feared there was no bravery in it.

IN TEL AVIV, Wu Ying tried to maintain an innocent expression as Israeli police led him into the government building. Air conditioning cooled his skin but failed to staunch the perspiration leaking from his pores.

He glanced at one of the officers and spoke in slow English. "What is this place?"

"Immigration offices."

The curt reply sent ice into his veins. "Am I going to be deported?"

"I can't say." The officer placed a hand on his handcuffs and directed him toward an elevator.

Once inside, the second officer pushed the button for the fifth floor. The door slid closed, sealing Wu Ying into an uncertain fate.

The elevator passed one floor after another, then dinged quietly as the door opened.

A light push on Wu Ying's back propelled him out into a corridor with at least a dozen office doors.

"To the right," his captor said in English.

They passed several doors before one of the officers hurried ahead and opened a door on the left.

Wu Ying stepped into small reception area. At one end, a receptionist worked at a window shielded in what he presumed was bullet-proof glass.

As they approached, she glanced up. Recognition flashed across her features as she saw the officers.

Without a word, she pressed a button on the side of her desk, and a loud click indicated that the door beside her had unlocked. The officers escorted Wu Ying through the doorway.

Inside, a row of chairs lined one wall. Opposite them stood several closed doors.

"Have a seat." The officer's words were clearly an order, not an invitation.

Wu Ying sat.

His escorts took the two seats beside him.

Obviously, he was going to be deported. What would happen to him when he was sent back to China?

Nothing good, that was for certain.

In the month since he'd been gone, the Chinese government had been pulling itself back together.

The downtrodden citizens had staged some uprisings, but the communists had overpowered the still unarmed populace. Horrific images had been publicly broadcast, depicting the punishment inflicted on the freedom fighters. The propaganda achieved its intended purpose of quelling the citizens' hope of overthrowing the tyrants.

Once again, the communists were winning in China.

Wu Ying sat motionless between his guards.

Things would go very badly for him in his native land. Not only had he gone AWOL from the military, but he had become a Christian.

And like his new friend Christian, he could expect only prison and torture after he was sent back to China.

Would he have the strength to endure?

He did not think so.

And yet, the very idea of renouncing his newfound faith – of denying Christ – filled him with the worst kind of horror.

3

The kremlin conference room hushed as a tall, thin man entered. Ivan had not seen President Dimitri Abramov in person since that terrifying day in the hospital. The meeting attendees respectfully rose to their feet as the Russian president strode to the head of the table. Silence fell as his sharp brown eyes swept the room, hesitating momentarily when they reached Ivan.

"Please be seated." President Abramov sat down, and everyone else followed his order.

"As you are all aware, the topic of this meeting is of utmost importance," he began. "Our country faces many challenges at this time, but we are also presented with a number of excellent opportunities. Following the vanquishing of our primary enemy, we may now move forward to either reclaim our historic colony in Alaska, or extend our influence in the Middle East."

The president paused. He eyed the military men gathered around the long table.

"I trust each of you will give your best advice in this matter, now that you have had time to conduct your final research and investigation. This morning's meeting is military only; this afternoon, we are convening with a component of leaders from government and civilian entities and military enterprises. Tomorrow, the government will meet to discuss and determine our future trajectory."

He turned to the man seated on his right. "General Gusev, we will hear your recommendation first."

The general stood to give his report, which seemed balanced and reflected some of Ivan's own thoughts on the matter. While Gusev allowed that either option was challenging, he leaned toward retaking Alaska.

Ivan found this encouraging, but he carefully watched Abramov's reaction. This president held more power than most of his predecessors, and he had been known to use it ruthlessly on occasion.

The president's façade did not reveal much as Gusev finished his statements, but even at this distance, Ivan thought he saw Abramov's left eye twitch slightly.

Was that from fatigue and stress, or was it from annoyance?

After Gusev took his seat, the president called on the next man at the table, and then the next, in the order they were seated. Most kept their summaries and recommendations shorter than five minutes, which kept the meeting moving at a good pace.

Ivan listened carefully to each report, while frequently glancing at President Abramov to catch his reaction. The man's face was a mask of indifference, but Ivan picked up a few tells that indicated his possible preference for moving into the Middle East.

Soon, the man beside him rose to give his recommendation. Ivan would be up next.

Should he stick to his plan to recommend seizing Alaska?

Or should he please the president with a recommendation favoring the Middle East?

In the end, his suggestions were only that – suggestions. The decision would officially be made by government leaders, who would certainly rubber-stamp the president's choice.

Too soon, the man beside him sat down, and the president's gaze fell on Ivan.

He struggled to his feet.

"Mister President." His gaze swept around the table. "Esteemed colleagues. The Ground Forces are prepared to meet any challenge, and I am highly confident of their likely success in either theatre, in combination with Aerospace and Navy forces, of course."

He paused momentarily. "It is my considered opinion that the Alaskan option would prove simple as far as enemy resistance, but somewhat challenging due to terrain. And of course, land access will be complicated due to the extensive tsunami damage to ports and harbors. Our troops can be transported by ships, or they can be airlifted, in some cases, onto Alaskan soil. Prior to this, our commandos could land amphibiously, preferably under cover of darkness, to secure landing sites for troop transport planes."

Ivan's gaze focused on President Abramov. The man's eye twitched.

"On the other hand," Ivan hurried to add, "the Israel option could open a glorious frontier for the federation, and the success of that venture would secure Russia's place of dominance over world affairs for a hundred years or more."

The president's jaw muscles relaxed, and his eyes gleamed.

Ivan continued. "For that option to be assured success, I would recommend a strong alliance with nations who share our perspective of the Middle East."

President Abramov's lip curled slightly. "Are you suggesting China?"

"Not at this time." Ivan drew a breath. "China proved an adequate ally against the United States, but it is now struggling to manage its own population. It also has its own ambitions and goals for the region, which do not necessarily align with ours. No, for this venture, I would suggest other allies."

The president leaned forward. "Such as?"

"Iran, Turkey and Syria. Possibly others, such as Egypt and Libya. Perhaps Kazakhstan and Uzbekistan. Perhaps even the Balkans."

President Abramov rubbed his thin grey mustache. "Regional allies, then."

"Yes." Ivan nodded. "A coalition of regional allies who are historically enemies of Israel, and who...." He paused to choose the right words. "Basically, allies who are more easily managed, who are already willing to accept Russian leadership. None of them can defeat Israel on their own, but each can contribute significantly in their own way and provide overland access for our Ground Forces."

President Abramov leaned back in his chair. He stared at Ivan.

Did he hate this idea?

Or was he open to it?

As he stepped out of the communications shack, Austin reached for Sierra's hand. She turned toward him and offered a faint smile.

"It'll be okay," she said. "It'll all work out."

"I hope you're right." He tightened, then relaxed, his grip

on her slender fingers. "I feel responsible to take care of my family. Grandpa especially, of course, but my cousins, too."

"How many might be coming here?"

"Only four. My cousin Rick and his wife, Sherry, and his brother Louis. And Grandpa."

"That's not so bad," she said quietly. "I mean, the upper islanders here have accommodated all the town residents already. What's four more people?"

He inhaled deeply. "You're sweet. But there are complicating factors."

"Such as?"

Austin led her away from their neighbors, guiding her into the dairy barn. The sweet smell of hay competed with the stench of manure.

"Such as, my grandpa needs help. He's got mild dementia, so he can't really be left alone. And my cousin Louis...." Austin drew a deep breath and looked at Sierra. "Louis is schizophrenic."

"Oh...." Her brow wrinkled as she fell silent.

"Maybe you know more about it than me, with your nursing training and all," he said.

"He needs to be medicated," Sierra pointed out.

"And maybe they've been able to get that for him, in Canada," Austin said. "But here? I'm pretty sure we don't have any drugs for that."

"Not unless there were some at the pharmacy." She squeezed his hand. "I can look in our inventory, but it's unlikely."

"Maybe someone here on the island was on medication for that," he suggested. "In which case, maybe the pharmacy did have some in stock."

"Maybe...." Doubt resounded in her tone.

"Can you check? Today?"

"Of course." She met his gaze. "I'll let you know what I find."

"You're the best." He pulled her close. "You know that, right?"

She smiled, and her eyes closed as he gave her a kiss.

SIERRA SAVORED THE SWEET KISS, which barely lasted a moment before Austin broke away. He took both of her hands in his.

"I'm thinking of making a trip out to my cabin."

"What?" She took a half-step back. "Why?"

"To see what's left of it, if anything."

"Why?" She asked again. "I mean, are you planning to move back there? What about being our pastor? It's too far to hike that distance all the time."

"I know." He rubbed his ear and gazed at the milk cows chewing their cud. "I was just thinking, if my cousins do come to Patmosa... maybe they could live out there."

"I don't see how," she objected.

"Well, I had a garden growing, and a greenhouse. I could walk out once a week, with some provisions."

"From the farm?"

He shrugged. "I guess."

"A lot of people won't like that." She tried again. "I mean, feeding farm produce to people who aren't helping grow it."

A pained look crossed his face. "I'm sure my cousins would be willing to help. But Sierra, my cousin is really schizo. When he gets off his drugs... he might be dangerous. He's paranoid, delusional and he could get violent. He can't be around people."

She released his hands. "So... you want to set up a psych ward for him at the far end of the island?"

He moistened his lips. "Obviously, I haven't had much time to think about this, but yeah. That's kind of where my mind was going."

"And your cousins? And grandpa? They'll live out there, too? Won't they be in danger from him?"

Austin's shoulders drooped. "Maybe."

"Not maybe." She waited until his eyes met hers. "For sure, Austin. When he's normal, Louis might love them all, but when his mental state fluctuates... he could stab them with a knife or something."

Austin sucked in a breath. He turned his gaze toward the cows.

Then, finally, he looked back at her.

"I don't know what to do, Sierra. I really don't know what to do."

She took his hand and gently ran her fingers over his knuckles. "But God will show you, right?"

"I hope so. Let's pray He does. Otherwise...." Austin didn't finish his thought, but Sierra understood the weight of his need.

"Let's pray now," she urged. "Together."

In the Tel Aviv immigration office, Wu Ying endured a long wait.

After what seemed like hours, one of the office doors before him opened, and a man appeared in the doorway.

"Mao Wu Ying."

He rose from his chair, his hands tingling in the cuffs

behind his back. No one offered to remove them, and Wu Ying dared not ask for that courtesy.

Both police officers accompanied him into the official's office. The Chinese man who had first knocked on Wu Ying's apartment door sat in a chair in the corner. He glanced up momentarily from his cell phone.

The immigration officer motioned to a chair in front of his desk.

"Please be seated."

Wu Ying sat awkwardly on the front of the chair, allowing space for his hands behind his back.

The official took his seat. "Please confirm that you are Mao Wu Ying."

"I am."

"You have been brought here today because of a lack of credibility in your asylum application, and also your failure to meet the criteria of the Refugee Convention."

Wu Ying had no response. He stared at the man who was dooming him to Hell on earth. Perhaps in his early thirties, the official was tall, even while seated, and wore his brown hair very short. Studious brown eyes peered at him though square eyeglasses.

"I was told you understand English," the man said.

"Yes."

"Do you understand what I have told you?"

"No." Wu Ying shook his head. "How am I not credible? How have I not met the conditions to be a refugee?"

He wanted to stand and shout his protest. This man was sending him to a terrible fate, and he acted as if it was a routine matter.

It wasn't. Not for Wu Ying.

His heart hammered his chest, but his body felt frozen.

"Your lack of credibility stems from your mis-statements

on your application for asylum." The man leaned forward and stared at Wu Ying. "You represented your involvement in the People's Liberation Army as a mid-level officer. Did you truly think we would not discover that you are a major general, at the very center of the command structure? You most likely issued the order to launch the nuclear weapons on our ally, the United States!"

"No." He gulped. "That is not true. I did not lie on my application!"

The man leaned back and crossed his arms. "Please. Entertain me with your explanation. I like a good story."

"It is true that I *was* a major general. However, I was demoted before the nuclear exchange. I was not involved in that."

"A likely story!" The official glanced from one police officer to the other before focusing on Wu Ying. "But please, tell us all about it."

So Wu Ying did.

He told of his arrest, and his release and demotion, and finally, the execution of his son. He hated sharing that heartbreak with these uncaring officials, but he hoped it might save him from the horrors awaiting him back in China.

Finally, the official ran his hand over his very short hair.

"That's quite a tale. Do you have any proof? Of any of it?"

"I have my demotion paperwork."

"If you are here as a spy, those documents could have been provided to you as a cover. What else do you have?"

Wu Ying couldn't think of anything. He felt every heartbeat as his mind raced to find an adequate response.

What could he possible say to save himself from deportation and the living hell that awaited him in his native country?

4

In the Siberian kremlin, Ivan stood on shaky legs as he waited for the president's response to his proposal.

"Please continue." President Abramov stared at him. "Your concept is an interesting one."

Ivan drew a quick breath. He had not been planning on this suggestion at all. In fact, until a few minutes ago, he'd been set on persuading the president to take back Alaska. But now, ideas he'd barely considered swirled in his mind and demanded to be announced to this audience.

"Thank you, sir. As I was saying, we could compile a coalition of regional partners whom I believe will enthusiastically support our efforts to conquer Israel. Each of them have their own motivation, obviously, but I expect they will jump at this opportunity to join us in overturning their most despised enemy."

He paused, then rushed on. "We already have some partnerships in the region. Iran, Syria... I'm convinced Turkey will join, and others will follow their lead."

The president appeared spellbound.

As more thoughts rolled into his mind, Ivan continued.

"Keep in mind, Israel's only true ally was the United States. The gazelle totally relied on the eagle to keep her enemies at bay. Now, the eagle is dead. Israel's protector is gone. Eventually, perhaps they'll find a new protector – but the iron is hot now. We need to strike. This is our best, and might be our only, opportunity to make this move. And I need not remind my esteemed colleagues in this room about Israel's recent gas and oil discoveries. If we could control that wealth, we would be rich for generations."

Around the room, heads nodded in agreement.

Ivan brought his point home. "If we can formalize our alliances with Israel's enemies, and conquer the Jews, we can finally bring lasting peace to the Middle East and immense wealth to Russia. Imagine the possibilities!"

Energy coursed through Ivan's veins. He hadn't felt this good since before his heart attack. In fact, he hadn't felt this good since he was in his thirties.

President Abramov continued staring at him, and Ivan sensed the man's mind was processing his ideas at the speed of light.

"I like this." The statesman rested both hands on the polished tabletop. "I like it very much. Let's hear what your colleagues have to say, and perhaps we can revisit this idea."

"Thank you, sir." Ivan sat down.

The general beside him stood to make his statements, and concluded with a supportive comment for Ivan's plan. The general who followed him did likewise. And so did General Pavlov, the eldest and most experienced military leader in the room.

Ivan could barely believe his good fortune. Less than an hour ago, he'd feared for his career and was coldly greeted by most of his colleagues, who certainly knew the score. Now, he was the rising star in this room.

If President Abramov decided to pursue his plan, he would present it to the civilian leaders, who would no doubt embrace it also.

Was it definitely the best course of action?

Ivan was sure it would be easier to take Alaska. The resistance there would be minimal.

Israel, on the other hand, would certainly put up a big fight. And while they were mum about their nuclear capabilities, everyone knew they maintained a nuclear arsenal of some sort, long assisted by their former ally, the United States.

It might not be easy to catch and destroy the Israeli gazelle.

But in the end, Ivan felt sure that with appropriate allies and their assorted strengths, the Russian bear would run her down.

IN PREPARATION for the hike out to his cabin, Austin gathered a few basic supplies in his backpack. He wanted to travel light, but he also wanted to be comfortable. Not to mention safe, if he had to spend the night in the forest with the bears.

He packed a water bottle and filter, a small pot with a lid, a folding knife, a fixed-blade knife, ferro rod, lightweight rain jacket and pants, small tarp, fishing hooks and line, map and compass, his handgun with the grizzly tooth gouges, and a rechargeable flashlight that he'd kept charged on a little solar panel. Since he had extra room in the bag, he added a small first-aid kit and a wool sweater.

As he swung the pack onto his back, a knock sounded on his door.

He opened it to find Sierra on his front step, holding a

vacuum-insulated food jar with a spoon, and a small package wrapped in old newspaper.

"I told Grandma what you were planning, and she sent a container of leek-potato soup and some smoked fish."

"Awesome. Thank you." He packed the food in his bag. "Please thank her for me."

"You want some company?" She turned those pretty hazel eyes on him. "I could join you."

He considered it for a moment before he shook his head. "Nah, I don't think that's a good idea. I might be gone overnight."

"Oh." A disappointed look crossed her features, and she glanced away. "Okay."

"Besides, I thought you were going to do something to get ready for your baptism."

Austin had never baptized anyone before, but Sierra and two other community members had been preparing for their baptisms when Pastor Parker died. As the new pastor, the task fell to him. The sacrament was scheduled later this summer, but Sierra had mentioned making some preparations today.

"Yeah, I guess." She looked into his eyes. "Be safe out there."

"Of course." He patted the revolver on his hip. "I've got some extra ammo and the Lord God."

She smiled. "Are you going to try to be back by seven o'clock? You told your cousin you'd be at the ham radio then."

"I doubt he's going to try to contact me again today, and probably not tomorrow." Austin focused on her. "But would you do me a favor and stand in if I'm not back? You can take a message, if he has any news."

"Okay. But try to be back."

"I will." He took her hand and kissed it gently. "See you soon."

WHEN AUSTIN LEFT, Sierra gathered cleaning supplies and headed to the cow pasture, where she emptied the water in the trough. Keeping an eye out for wayward cattle, she climbed into the slimy trough with a long-handled scrub brush and a nearly-empty bottle of dish soap. Her boots skidded on the slippery bottom, but she grabbed the rim and remained upright.

"Gross," she announced to the distant cows. "This is disgusting."

She dribbled some dish soap on her scrub brush and jabbed at the green algae, scrubbing it for a solid half hour.

"Hey, cousin!" McKenna's cheery voice re-directed her attention. The pretty newlywed was making her way across the pasture. "I don't think the cows care all that much."

Careful to avoid slipping, Sierra stood up. "It's not for the cows. It's for me."

McKenna's blonde brows shot up. "How's that?"

"We're using this for the baptism."

"Ah...." McKenna grinned. "So you don't want to get dunked in the Pacific?"

"I'd probably keel over from hyperthermia before you could fish me out." Sierra shook the brush over the daisies growing next to the trough. She focused on McKenna. "Where did you get baptized?"

"In town. The Baptist church had a baptistry there."

"Oh. That must have been nice."

Hideaway's First Baptist church building had been destroyed in the tsunami.

McKenna plucked a daisy and stuck it in her hair. "It was. But yours will be so... memorable."

She laughed as Sierra lunged at her with the wet scrub brush, soaking her elbow. "Hey, be nice!"

Sierra's momentum carried her a bit farther than she expected, and she slipped on the slimy bottom of the trough. Before she could squeak, she landed hard.

Pain zapped her hips and traveled up her spine.

"Ow!" She blinked up at the cloudy sky.

"Are you alright?" Concern widened McKenna's blue eyes. She extended a hand to help her up.

"I'll be okay." Sierra accepted the hand up, moving slowly as she got her feet under her. "I think I'm about done here, anyway."

McKenna clutched her arm and assisted her out of the slippery trough. "I'm not sure using this as a baptismal tank is such a good idea. Can't they just sprinkle you or something? That's what Catholics do, right?"

"I wanna be dunked," Sierra explained. "I want the full experience."

Still clutching the scrub brush, she looked to the sky and raised her arms toward Heaven. "Wash over me, Holy Spirit!"

McKenna smiled. "You've changed, you know that?"

"I hope so." Sierra focused on her cousin. "Truly. I've got a long ways to go still, but I want to be a new person. I'm not too proud of my old self."

McKenna linked arms with her, and they started for the cattle gate. "You weren't so bad. A little rough around the edges...."

"No, I was pretty bad. Still am, sometimes. But I'm on the right road now." She pulled her damp pants away from the backs of her thighs. "Oh, this is so disgusting!"

"Sierra...." McKenna's voice was subdued, and she stopped walking. "I actually came to find you because I need to tell you something."

"Anything." Sierra paused as she noted her cousin's serious expression. "What? What is it?"

SEATED in the immigration official's office at the Ministry of the Interior, Wu Ying felt his face grow warm despite the air conditioning freely flowing through the ceiling vents. Was it possible to prove any of his story? How?

His mind landed on an idea, and he began to speak before he thought it through.

"I have a friend...." He paused. Should he draw Christian into this? What if Wu Ying's mention of Christian resulted in his and Wei Min's deportation also?

"A friend?" The immigration officer leaned forward and folded his hands on his desk. "Who is this friend? Can they corroborate your story?"

Wu Ying froze. He should not have mentioned his friends. Now they, also, would be in danger.

He swallowed hard. "No, I do not think so."

"Then why did you bring them up?" The official's brown eyes stared at him, unblinking. "Do they have any knowledge of this?"

Wu Ying tried to appear nonchalant. Christian could provide a witness to Wu Ying's brief incarceration during the war, and to his desperate escape from the country.

On the other hand, Christian and Wei Min's association with him could result in their deportation to China. He could never live with himself if he caused such a thing. In an instant, he chose his friends' wellbeing over his own.

He shrugged. "Mostly what I have told him. The same I have told you."

"That won't help you. Only evidence will help you." The

man's eyebrows lowered. He gazed at Wu Ying for a long moment. "Why do I have the impression that you are hiding something?"

Wu Ying met his gaze. Over the decades in a communist country, he had grown strong in the art of deception. He felt bad deploying it now, but his only motive was to save Christian and Wei Min from a terrible fate, so he hoped God would forgive him for this.

"I have nothing to hide," he said flatly. "If you do not believe my story and my documents, I suppose you will deport me."

The official tilted his head. "Yes. I believe we will."

Panic rushed into Wu Ying's mind, and he tried to calm it.

He couldn't go back to China and the horrors that awaited there. He just couldn't!

The immigration officer focused on him.

"You will be here in our office for a while. If you won't cause any trouble, I'll have your handcuffs removed."

"Thank you," Wu Ying responded stiffly. "It would be foolish to cause trouble, so I will not do it."

"Very well." The official turned to the police officers. "Please remove the cuffs and take him out."

Wu Ying rose from his chair. An officer keyed his handcuffs and took them off. Wu Ying rubbed his wrists. He eyed the immigration official behind the desk.

"Please, can you tell me... will I be deported immediately?"

"That depends."

"On what?" A glimmer of hope illuminated his dark fears.

The man turned to his computer screen. "On what we find out."

5

As the meeting in the conference room came to a close, a buoyancy lifted Ivan's spirits. Russia still had a bright future, despite the terrible blows she'd suffered at the hands of the Americans. And now that the United States held no significance in the world, the Russian Federation faced opportunities unlike she'd seen in a hundred years.

This was his country's moment, and he was back at work, in the thick of it all.

"Major General Orlov." The president's voice drew his attention to the head of the table. "A number of federation leaders will be gathering this afternoon. I hope you'll be prepared to give them an overview of your suggestion."

Ivan gave a single nod. "It may not be fully developed, but I would be happy to present the general concept."

"Good." President Abramov's gaze swept the other generals. "I'll ask the rest of you to begin conferring with Major General Orlov and his staff to prepare detailed plans for a full military mobilization into the Middle East."

He paused. "Obviously, nothing will be settled before the

government makes its decision, but I expect you all to make this your first priority at this time. Whatever is decided, we will want to act expeditiously and at the earliest possible time. I'm sure you all understand this window of opportunity will be short."

The president rose from his chair. "That is all for now."

The generals rose in unison, and Ivan stood with them until the president had exited the room. As soon as their leader had exited, the men began gathering around Ivan

The eldest general spoke first.

"Your idea is a fascinating one." General Pavlov's old eyes twinkled. "You must have been dreaming this up during your two months away from work."

Ivan smiled. "The first month I was in a coma."

"Your mind was very busy." Pavlov patted Ivan's shoulder. "Now, you have created much work for the rest of us. I'll need to get my staff started on new contingency planning and logistics. But I must say, having a strong regional coalition could be the key to our success. You've outdone yourself, Ivan Alexandrovich Orlov."

"That means a great deal, coming from you. Thank you."

As the elder general turned away, younger ones pressed closer. For twenty minutes, they offered suggestions, plied Ivan with questions, and roundly congratulated his plan.

Finally, they hurried away to begin briefing their staff, and Colonel Lev Balakin approached.

"You made a remarkable comeback today," the subordinate man said.

Ivan smiled, sensing the double meaning in the colonel's statement. A physical return, obviously, but a leadership rebound, as well. He picked up the red folder.

"Thank you for your memoranda. It was very helpful."

Ivan turned away from the conference table and started for the door.

"Sir?" The colonel's voice carried a note of surprise. "Isn't that your walker? Don't you rely on it?"

Ivan glanced back at the contraption. Until this moment, he hadn't given it a thought – but he'd been on his feet for over twenty minutes without any assistance or weakness, and now he was walking like a teenager.

He turned to the colonel. "I guess I don't need it anymore."

The younger man blinked but said nothing as Ivan strode out of the room.

As Ivan neared his office, he marveled at his rapid recovery. Until an hour ago, he was unable to walk without the device. His doctor had said he would need it for some time, and then use a cane until he fully recovered.

But now, he felt as strong as he ever had.

His steps were almost jaunty as he walked into his office, set the folder on his desk, and stretched his back.

He felt good. Really good.

Perhaps there was no medical explanation for that. Maybe it was due to being back at work, in his element, impressing the president and his colleagues – maybe those good emotional feelings created good physical ones.

In any case, he wasn't going to waste time in wonderment.

He had a lot of work to do in preparation for this afternoon's meeting.

AUSTIN STRODE AWAY THE FARM, entering the forest on the old logging road that he and Sierra had hiked when they escaped the tsunami.

Movement in his peripheral vision registered a moment before something cold and damp bumped his hand.

Reflexively, he stepped sideways and reached for the gun on his hip as his gaze shot to the cold, wet intruder.

A Belgian Malinois dog looked up at him.

"Major!" Austin could barely believe it. "What are you doing here?"

Since Ian Parker died, Major had stood watch at the pastor's front door constantly, rain or shine, waiting for his master to return. Austin had fed and brushed him every day, but this was the first time he'd seen Major leave the empty parsonage with the big dog house on the porch.

Major gave a single wag of his tail, then looked down the road.

"You coming with me?" Austin asked. "I could use the company, to be honest."

The dog glanced at him, then took a step forward.

"Awesome. I'm glad you're coming along." He dropped his hand to the dog's shoulders and gave him a pat. "I think it'll be good for you, too."

Having a dog on the hike could be helpful, as Major might see or smell predators before Austin could see them. Plus, it was nice not being alone – while also not pressed for conversation, as he might be with a human companion.

Major trotted ahead, looked over his shoulder at Austin, then continued up the overgrown logging trail.

"I hope you know where you're going," Austin joked. "I don't want to have to go searching for you if you get lost."

He adjusted his backpack straps and hurried after the dog. It would be nice to get out to his cabin site, see what, if anything, remained, and be home again by dark. This should be possible, as long as he didn't get lost or have to spend hours in a tree, waiting for a bear to leave his vicinity.

Honestly, he didn't expect to find much. His cabin had been built above a small cove, but the mega-tsunami had come up the Inside Passage with incredible strength and fury. The cabin had almost certainly been caught up and swept out to sea, along with all of his books and most of his belongings.

He doubted he'd find anything intact at his homesite, but he needed to make this trip to be sure.

Fellowship Farm owned some small drones, but they were too important to risk flying out across the forest to the far side of the island – they were likely to be blown down into the trees somewhere and lost. So, this was the best way to find out what, if anything, remained of his home.

Plus, the quiet walk alone might help clear his head. He needed to figure out what to do about his cousins and grandfather.

The truth was, he felt bad about bringing such needy and possibly dangerous people to the island. The community already struggled to survive day by day. They didn't need more trouble.

On the other hand, these were Austin's relatives, and he felt responsible for them. Especially for Grandpa.

Louis was probably more of Rick's responsibility, since they were brothers.

But the family was hanging together, and they were on their way here, if they could make it.

Austin swiped at a mosquito on the back of his arm.

How would they get here, really? The community only had two viable fishing boats. The port communities Rick mentioned were a long way from Patmosa Island.

Even if Austin could borrow a boat to retrieve his family, where would he get the fuel for it?

He might have a couple of gallons of gas left in his pickup, but even if he drained the tank and used it in a boat, that wouldn't take him very far.

A sailboat might work. But he didn't know anybody who had one.

Major trotted back to him and nuzzled his hand.

"You're a good boy, Major." He gave the dog a pat.

Honestly, this situation was impossible. His family was about to be evicted from Canada, but there was no realistic way he could retrieve them – and no safe way for them to live here on the island if he could.

He stopped walking, then looked up at the cloudy sky. "Lord, what should I do?"

A quiet silence answered him.

Austin sighed and continued his hike.

STANDING IN THE CATTLE PASTURE, Sierra stared at her cousin. McKenna looked away, as if trying to find the words to tell her some big news. Was it good? Bad? Had she had a fight with Tristan? Had someone died?

Sierra gripped McKenna's arm. "What? Tell me."

Her cousin's blue eyes misted as she turned them to Sierra. Her mouth contorted slightly.

"I...." She gulped, then started again. "I'm late."

"For what?" A sudden realization sank into her. "Late? You're late? You mean, your cycle?"

McKenna nodded.

"What? Are you pregnant?" Sierra dropped her scrub brush and took both of McKenna's hands. "You're going to have a baby?"

"I don't know yet." McKenna hauled in a breath.

"How late are you?"

"Not very." She looked away. "About a week."

"That's not very long." Sierra suddenly wished she'd paid more attention in her maternity nursing course. "Um... maybe you're not even pregnant. It's too soon to know."

"I know, but...." McKenna's lower lip quivered. "I don't know whether to be happy or scared." The blonde girl stared at her. "A baby," she whispered. "In these times? No hospital, no doctor."

McKenna focused hard on her. "Only you."

"Me?" Now it was Sierra's turn to panic. "Oh, no, not just me."

Her mind raced. "First, this is probably a false alarm. You'll probably get your period. Second, if you *are* pregnant, which you probably aren't, then we'll have time to find a real doctor. Or a real nurse. Or a midwife. Something!"

McKenna stepped forward, falling into Sierra's arms. "I'm scared."

She patted her cousin's back.

"It's okay." She did her best to sound reassuring. "It'll all be okay."

Her mind raced to the bookshelf in her bedroom. Did she have any nursing textbooks on maternity care? She needed to learn a world's worth of information on gynecology and obstetrics, and she was pretty sure she'd rented those books and returned them. Or she may have had digital texts, in which case she probably couldn't access them anymore.

As she hugged her cousin, she scolded herself for being so unprepared. Hard-copy books on important topics were an absolute necessity now, and she had so few!

ACCORDING TO HIS WATCH, Wu Ying had been seated in the hall outside the immigration official's office for less than thirty minutes when the lock on the door behind him clicked. He glanced back to see who was entering.

Escorted by a police officer, Wei Min walked in first, her hands in cuffs behind her back. Her expression was stoic, but her face was a shade paler than normal.

Behind her, an officer pushed Christian in his wheelchair.

Their gaze settled on Wu Ying, and the puzzlement in their faces cleared. He was at the center of their new trouble.

His chest tightened. He had tried not to involve them, but here they were, and so soon!

How?

Easily, with modern technology. Geo-fencing, for one. The cell phones of asylum seekers were registered, and they were required to carry them any time they left their residence.

Wu Ying often met with Christian and Wei Min, so obviously all those visits would be easily accessible through phone tracking.

Also, they had arrived on the same flight from China. And they attended church together, as well.

It would not have been at all difficult for the authorities to connect them, and with Wu Ying's accidental blunder today in mentioning a friend... he hung his head, hoping he had not doomed them to a return to China and the torture that awaited them there.

Wei Min was escorted directly into the official's office, while Christian was wheeled to the end of the row of chairs where Wu Ying waited.

Christian met his gaze. He made the sign of the cross, then folded his hands in prayer and looked expectantly toward the ceiling before glancing again at Wu Ying.

Oxygen rushed into Wu Ying's lungs. He nodded in response to his friend's encouragement to pray.

He should have been doing that from the beginning, instead of panicking and making things worse.

Folding his hands in his lap, he let his gaze fall to the floor.

Oh, Father. Please help us. Please save my friends from my mistakes. I pray that you will somehow save us all... again. In the holy name of Jesus, amen.

Peace replaced some of his panic, and he recalled that just last night, he had read the 139th chapter of Psalms, and had committed verses seven through ten to memory.

Now, when he needed them, they returned to his mind.

"Where can I go from Your Spirit?
Or where can I flee from Your presence?
If I ascend into heaven, You are there;
If I make my bed in hell, behold, You are there.
If I take the wings of the morning,
And dwell in the uttermost parts of the sea,
Even there Your hand shall lead me,
And Your right hand shall hold me."

No matter where he went – even if he was deported to China – he would not be alone. The Lord would be with him and uphold him.

6

Ivan sent a flurry of emails to his staff, then made several phone calls. He needed all Ground Forces leaders to be aware of his suggested plan, and to provide input on the best way to implement it. Also, he wanted them to be ready to prepare for this theater of operations, should the government approve it.

He ate lunch at his desk, reading emails and compiling notes for the meeting.

There wasn't time to prepare a slick, polished presentation. He'd have to wow his audience with spoken facts, figures and information, rather than charts, graphs and computer graphics. Today, he'd be going old-school. Back to the early days in his career, when computers were more novel and less ubiquitous.

In those days, Russia had struggled to regain her footing after the disintegration of the Soviet Union. They had been hard years, filled with difficulty and some humiliation for the Russian Federation. But they'd built a foundation of strong, dedicated men who would stop at nothing to see Russia return to her deserved status and glory.

Ivan was one of the youngest of those men, and he put his heart into his work. Which likely contributed to his cardiac issues, but those were resolved, at least for now. He would take his statins and follow his doctor's orders, and hopefully live to see a half-dozen grandchildren someday.

His thoughts flitted to his children. Anton remained distant and defiant following the death of his foolish girlfriend, while sweet Nina struggled to adjust to life in Siberia. She seemed to enjoy attending Sunday services at the cathedral, though – or at least she enjoyed dressing up for them.

This upcoming military venture might prove very advantageous to his children and their children after them. If Russia found success in the Middle East, she could become amazingly wealthy. Perhaps more wealthy than America had been before she'd been knocked off her pinnacle of power.

In fact, his own children might benefit more than others, given that this form of the expedition had been his own brainchild. If it proved successful, Anton and Nina would find every door open for them. They would have a friend in every corner, a boost at every opportunity. Life would be very good for the Orlovs.

But only if Ivan's military plan worked as well as he hoped. No, not hoped... envisioned.

If things went wrong – if his plan failed – then Ivan and Marina would become social and professional outcasts. Their children would be doomed to derision. Life would be hard for several generations of Orlovs.

He shuddered.

That wouldn't happen. It couldn't.

And to make sure it wouldn't, he would make certain that every contingency was covered. If this plan was to move forward, it must succeed in spectacular fashion.

His phone rang.

President Abramov's assistant spoke quickly. "To accommodate the large number of attendees, this afternoon's meeting has been moved to the ballroom on the third floor. Unfortunately, the elevator is out of service. Will you need assistance with the stairs?"

Ivan balked, but only for a minute.

"No. I will be fine. Thank you."

After he hung up the phone, he reconsidered. Two long flights of stairs? Without any crutches or help?

This morning, there was no way he could have managed that.

Now, he could only hope his sudden physical improvement would hold out for the remainder of the day. Because at the end of it, he would have to descend those stairs, again without assistance, when he would likely be fatigued or exhausted.

SIERRA HELD the cattle gate open for her cousin, then secured it behind them. She focused on McKenna.

"What did Tristan say?"

McKenna averted her eyes. "I haven't told him yet."

"What? You told me first?" She clutched at her heart in mock astonishment. "Seriously, though, why haven't you said anything to him?"

"Lots of reasons." Her cousin hung her head. "It's only been a week, like you said. I'm probably not even pregnant. And... well... we were going to wait a while – a long time – before we had kids."

"That sounds like a good plan, since you've only been married for about two months!" Sierra tried to take the sting out of her tone as she added, "But if you don't get your period soon, you should tell him."

"I know."

"In fact, you should just tell him now."

McKenna blinked "Why? You think it's really... you think I'm pregnant?"

"Maybe you are, maybe you're not. But you should have told him first, before anyone."

"But you're almost a nurse. And my cousin. My confidant."

Sierra looped her arm through McKenna's. "We'll always be tight. But you married Tristan. He's your confidant now."

The newlywed sighed. "I don't know how he'll take it."

"He'll probably be shocked, then excited."

"Then scared," McKenna added. "That was my sequence, anyway."

"You should tell him not to take it too seriously until you're farther along. You might get your period, or have a miscarriage, or –"

"What?" McKenna yanked her to a halt. "Why would you say that?"

"It's not uncommon in the first trimester." Sierra tried to use her soothing tone. "That's one reason why lots of couples don't tell people until the mother-to-be is starting to show. Once you're in your second trimester, you're likely to carry to term."

McKenna swallowed. "That's sad."

"Carrying to term?"

"No!" McKenna scowled at her. "Miscarriage. Losing a child."

"Yeah, it is." Sierra nodded. "Very sad."

They sighed in unison, then continued on toward the newlyweds' tiny home.

"He built it for the two of us," McKenna reminded her.

"We figured one day, when we were ready to start a family, we'd add on to our little love nest."

"A baby doesn't take much room," Sierra pointed out. "Especially nowadays. It's not like you'll be flooded with gifts and toys and baby furniture. All you'll need is a crib."

"And a rocker." McKenna's eyes sparkled. "I definitely want a rocker."

They stopped at the front steps.

"So, you're going to tell him now?" Sierra asked.

"Soon," her cousin hedged.

"Today, though?"

McKenna shrugged and glanced away.

Sierra squeezed her cousin's arm. "You have to tell him today. Don't put it off. Promise me."

A weak smile lifted McKenna's lips. "Okay. I will."

AFTER A LONG AND STRENUOUS HIKE, Austin finally approached the crest of the mountain. From the top, he would be able to see "his" side of the island, although he likely wouldn't see his cabin site, due to the evergreen trees that had survived the mega-tsunami.

Major trotted ahead, his nose to the ground. Suddenly he stopped, lifted his head, and froze.

"What is it, boy?" Austin asked quietly.

The dog glanced back at him, then stared into the forest.

"You see something?"

Major lifted one front paw. His ears turned straight ahead.

Austin instinctively reached for his handgun. "What is it?"

The dog's shoulders relaxed, followed by the rest of his body. He turned and trotted to Austin.

"Good boy. You let me know if you see any bears, okay?"

The Belgian Malinois panted, then trotted up the trail.

Austin followed, soon breaking out of the dense forest onto a rocky outcropping. He approached the edge. The sun broke free of the clouds and brightened the Inside Passage, bringing out its deepest blue tones. Somewhere down there lay Austin's property – and maybe some of his belongings.

His stomach grumbled and he considered eating the soup and fish Mrs. Forrester had sent – but he decided to wait and eat at his cabin site. He'd sit and rest and soak in his surroundings.

Perhaps the cabin could be rebuilt. His cousins could work on that, and then move in once the roof was up.

Austin started down the slope, then realized the dog was gone.

"Major?" He drew in a deep breath and yelled louder. "Major!"

In the distance, ferns whipped as they were disturbed, and soon the dog's ears appeared, followed by the rest of his lithe, muscular body. He bounded across the terrain, racing toward Austin.

"That's a good boy." He gave the dog a pat. "Let's go see if anything's left of my cabin."

As they descended toward the water, ducking under branches and scrambling over downed trees, Austin considered how on earth he might get his cousins here.

Everything that once seemed normal was now preposterous – planes, helicopters, ferries – all were out of the question. Even a standard fishing boat was almost beyond the realm of possibility, because there was no fuel.

He kept coming back to the idea of a sailboat.

Austin knew nothing of sailing.

He wasn't even sure he knew anyone on the island who

sailed. Did anyone ever sail in the Inside Passage? Perhaps it was too dangerous.

But he doubted that – for thousands of years, people had sailed all kinds of places. Many lives were lost to sea. Even the Apostle Paul had been shipwrecked following a very long and terrible storm.

If Austin could find a sailboat to buy or hire, would he be able to bring his four relatives to Patmosa Island?

The mayor was staunchly opposed to that, and if Austin knew Mayor Williams, the man was at this very moment rallying people to his side of the argument. That's what he did. A true politician, he wasted no time cajoling, gaslighting and persuading folks to see things his way.

And it would not be difficult for Jake Williams to convince them.

Nobody really wanted any more people to move to the island – unless they were one's own friends or family, of course. But other peoples' relatives? Or total strangers?

No way.

They would just be more mouths to feed, when there was too little food already.

He imagined the farm taking a vote. He would almost certainly lose.

So, what could he do? He felt responsible to care for Grandpa. Austin was his guardian and power of attorney – although those formal designations probably didn't matter much these days.

If the community voted to bar his family members from settling here, what could he do?

As he saw it, there were two options in that case. Either tell his family they couldn't come, and continue living his life on Patmosa, or else join his family in another location so he could care for Grandpa.

If they could get to a town with a functional airport, perhaps they could all fly to Bolivia, where Austin's dad lived.

He stopped and wiped the perspiration from his forehead. He'd never been to Bolivia, and he wasn't too excited about going there now.

Besides, what about Sierra?

Their relationship was beginning to blossom. Would he leave her here in Alaska and wish her well? Would she be willing to leave her friends and family to move to South America with him?

He clenched his jaw. This whole situation was nuts. What a crazy predicament!

IN THE SLEEK, modern Ministry of the Interior office, Wu Ying looked up as the immigration official's door opened and Wei Min stepped out, escorted by a police officer.

Her hands were still shackled, and her gaze did not lift off the grey carpet under her feet.

Wu Ying's heart grew heavy. This was his fault. If only he had not mentioned any friends!

Her escort steered her to the end of the row of chairs. "Be seated."

"Can't you remove her handcuffs?" Wu Ying implored. "Obviously she is no threat."

Even by Chinese averages, Wei Min was a small woman. Any of the men in the waiting room were twice her size, with the exception of her brother, who had finally begun to gain a little weight.

No one responded to Wu Ying's plea, but Wei Min sent him a grateful glance as she eased awkwardly into a chair.

Christian's guard wheeled him forward, through the immigration officer's doorway. A moment later, the door closed.

Wu Ying wanted to ask Wei Min a hundred questions about her time in that little office, but he dared not. Their captors stood by, ready to misinterpret every word. Perhaps his analysis of the situation was tainted by his decades under communism – perhaps it was different here in Israel – but he didn't know and he could not depend on that hope.

For her part, Wei Min remained silent, her gaze resting on the carpet.

Behind the closed door, voices raised in volume. Not Christian's voice, but the Chinese Israeli officer and another man – either the police officer or the immigration official.

Why would they be upset?

It seemed unlikely Christian could have angered them. He was such a kind, innocent soul.

Were they arguing amongst themselves, then?

The door opened suddenly. The Chinese man, looking quite irritated, beckoned to Wu Ying. "Please come in for a moment."

Wu Ying stood and started forward. His feet seemed to move of their own accord, carrying him to some untimely demise.

Christian gazed up at him as he entered.

"Please sit," the man ordered in Chinese.

Wu Ying took the seat in front of the desk where he had previously sat. The immigration official shot him a dark look.

"Please tell me how you met this man." He gestured toward Christian. "In English, please."

"When I was in jail, he was my cellmate," Wu Ying explained.

Surely Christian had told the same story. What could be so controversial or unbelievable about that?

Disbelief darkened the official's face. "This man claims to

have been a sewer worker. His sister said she was a janitor at a meat-processing facility. You are a major general in the PLA. And yet, you all arrived together and have been in constant contact with each other here in Israel."

The man stared at Wu Ying as if expecting an explanation.

"I know little about their former occupations," he answered.

"Occupations? If what you all say is true, you practically lived in different worlds!" He glared at Wu Ying. "A Chinese major general would not associate with such common people."

"Ordinarily, I would agree. To my shame." He gave the official a steady gaze. "However, you must agree these were not ordinary circumstances. I was jailed and tortured, then demoted. This man was kind to me."

Wu Ying paused to consider his next words. "Here in Israel, there are few persons from China. Why would we not remain in contact here? In a culture that is so foreign to us, we share language and customs, food and heritage."

He intentionally left out their religious connection. Christianity was not embraced in Israel. It was not outlawed, exactly, but many Jews wished that it would be.

Only two percent of Israel's population was Christian, and over three-quarters of those believers were Arab.

The immigration official rubbed his chin, then crossed his arms. He gazed evenly at Wu Ying.

"Please return to your seat in the hall. If I need more information, I'll call you back in."

Wu Ying rose and trudged back to the row of chairs. Wei Min shot him a questioning glance, but he had no answers.

The best he could do was shrug.

7

Ivan did not make an effort to be early for the afternoon meeting with the oligarchs of government and civilian entities and military enterprises. Instead, he worked on his presentation until the last possible minute, then made his way up the stairs with very little trouble and entered the ballroom moments before the meeting was to be called to order.

At first glance, he guessed three hundred chairs had been brought in for the meeting, and all were claimed. Many faces turned toward him as he entered near the front of the room. Excited whispers were exchanged between the attendees. Clearly, rumors of his plan of attack had made the rounds, and had earned some enthusiastic interest.

He felt like a celebrity.

As he glanced around, President Abramov's aide made his way toward Ivan.

"You'll be seated here in the front, at the speaker's table," the man said.

"Thank you." Ivan spotted his name on a placard, just to the right of President Abramov's seat.

How things had changed since this morning, when he'd been banished to the foot of the table!

Moments later, the president arrived and the room fell silent.

President Abramov called the meeting to order, made some introductory statements, then called on Ivan to present his plan.

Ivan rose. He spoke animatedly for about thirty minutes, summarizing all the details he'd been able to compile during his brief preparatory time. Then he took questions for another half an hour.

The entire time, he remained on his feet without any problems at all.

Finally, the president thanked him for his presentation and asked him to remain until the close of the meeting, in case the leaders had additional questions.

President Abramov then presented the original options – Alaska or Israel – and a summary for each.

"We must be thorough in our deliberations on this most serious matter," he reminded the assembly. "At the same time, we must be expeditious. Our window of time is short, as other nation states no doubt are forming their own plans as we speak. I would urge you to investigate these options completely, and return your input as soon as possible."

He glanced at Ivan.

"I would like to thank Major General Ivan Orlov for his creative suggestion and his insightful presentation this afternoon. As most of you know, he has been ill and today is his first day back at work."

Ivan smiled and thanked the president as the room resounded with applause. It continued until he rose to his feet and acknowledged their support.

He was not accustomed to such popular acclaim. Most of

his work was done quietly, in the background, and was only recognized among the military leadership.

"Thank you. Thank you." He smiled at the audience and raised his hands to quiet them. "Thank you very much."

He took his seat, feeling a warmth in his face. The recognition and applause felt good. It felt very good, and he realized he could get accustomed to it.

Perhaps, if this military conquest proved successful, he would consider a life in politics. Only at the highest levels, of course.

Maybe he could be president one day. He had excellent leadership skills, and it wasn't like he would be the first military leader to move into civilian leadership.

It was a crazy thought. He'd never had any real interest in politics. He was a warrior.

Even now, he recognized that it wasn't politics that he found appealing. It was the approval and recognition of the crowd.

As Austin reached the lower slopes of the island and approached his cabin site, he stared though the foliage, trying to see what might remain of his home.

If it weren't for the map and compass, he might have doubted his location. Nothing looked familiar, other than vague contours of the land. Instead of a healthy forest, trees were down all over the ground. Some leaned over or across each other, like a gigantic game of pick-up sticks.

He'd have years' worth of overturned timber to clean up if he ever moved back out here.

Finally, his cove came into view, along with his cabin site.

It was a wreck.

He could make out the corner locations of his cabin only because the posts and piers remained.

Major trotted down to the site and snuffled around.

The garden was now a mud flat covered in forest debris. There was no sign of the greenhouse. Even the wood-fired hot tub was gone without a trace.

The mega-tsunami had hit his home as hard as he'd imagined, sweeping everything out to the briny waters of the Inside Passage.

Austin sank onto a downed tree trunk and surveyed the scene.

His property was a diluvian disaster. Even the outhouse was gone, and its pit was now filled with soil and debris.

Near the location of his erstwhile greenhouse, something small and red caught his attention. He focused on it.

His teakettle?

He pushed himself off the log and walked over to check it out.

It was his teakettle, alright. The handle had been snagged on a tree branch. Austin pulled it free and checked it over. A small dent marred the metal near the top of the kettle, but otherwise, it was fine.

His gaze swept the rest of the area. The dog scrambled over downed trees and trotted along a log. He was truly agile.

Suddenly, Major tilted his head, swiveled his ears forward, and hopped off the log. He darted forward a few feet, then scooted through some of the branches that braced the tree above the forest floor.

He whined, then appeared to be trying to pull something out from under the tree.

"What is it, boy?" Austin cocked his head and started toward the dog.

Major obviously had something in his jaws and was trying to yank it out from the branches' clutches.

"I hope you haven't found a bear cub. Or a porcupine." He paused. "Or a skunk!"

The possibilities were endless, but not very good.

"Leave it, Major."

The dog froze, as if he knew that command – but then he went on tugging on his treasure.

"Oh, good heavens." Austin cautiously approached. "What is it?"

If it had been a live skunk or porcupine, Major would have dropped it by now. Most likely, it was some dead critter – but there was no stench, so either the creature had just died, or it had been dead long enough that it didn't smell bad anymore.

Major leaned back on his haunches, using leverage to free his entangled prize. As it loosened, he scrambled backward, pulling it through the downed tree's branches. He gave it another yank, and it came free.

It appeared to be a muddy board.

"A board?" Austin scratched his head. "You went to all that effort to pull out a board?"

Major panted and sat on his haunches, eyeing Austin.

"Well, you got a dirty board. Congratulations. I got a tea kettle." Austin chuckled. "I guess we've both had a real profitable day."

He glanced at the board. It might have come from his cabin or outbuildings, or the tsunami may have swept it in from elsewhere.

"Okay buddy, I think we should head home." Austin hooked the kettle to the outside of his backpack with a carabiner.

Major stood, whined and tugged on his board.

Austin shook his head. "I don't think you want to drag that all the way back home."

The dog sat down by his prize.

"Seriously, Major, just leave it there. Or bring it with you. I don't care."

Major tilted his head and looked at Austin.

"You should get a stick or something. They're easier to carry." Austin approached the dog. "What's the deal with the board, anyway?"

He picked it up, knocked off the dried mud, and turned it over.

Dark lettering emerged as Austin wiped it off.

Alone with God. For God alone.

He stared at the sign that had hung over his picture window. As a hermit living out here, it was his personal motto.

Of all the things in his cabin, only two possessions survived the tsunami – his tea kettle and his motto. And he wouldn't have found the board, either, but Major was determined to pull it from the downed tree's branches.

Austin looked toward heaven.

"Lord? Is this some kind of sign?"

As Sierra walked to the ham radio building, she glanced toward the old logging road. It was nearly seven p.m., and Austin wasn't back yet. Hopefully his family wouldn't try to contact him this evening, but she'd agreed to cover for him.

He'd said he might not return until tomorrow, but she hoped he'd make it back before dark. He would probably be fine if he had to spend the night in the forest. But of course, there were bears out there, and he was alone.

Not totally alone. God was with him. But still... she'd sleep better knowing he was home safe, instead of hanging out with the grizzly bears.

The radio operator looked up as she entered.

Alfred's wizened eyebrows lifted slightly. "Where's Austin?"

"He hiked out to his property. I said I'd stand by for him, in case his family checks in. Have you heard anything from them?"

"Not yet." He glanced at the wall clock. "Still a bit early."

She eased into the chair beside him. "How long have you been a ham?"

"More than forty years now."

Sierra surveyed his radio gear. It looked about that old. Not that she would know what newer ham equipment looked like, but none of this stuff looked modern.

He glanced at her. "You going to the meeting this evening?"

She turned her full attention on him. "There's a meeting?"

"At seven thirty. The mayor called it. Something about newcomers to the island."

Sierra's dinner turned sour in her stomach. "I'll bet it's about Austin's family."

"That was my thought, as well." He eyed her. "You might want to attend."

"You bet I do." She closed her mouth to avoid saying something she might regret.

The mayor had no business calling a meeting about Austin's family while he was away from the farm and unable to defend himself or make his rebuttal.

Jake Williams was a low-down scoundrel!

One of these days, he would get what was coming to him.

WAITING IN THE IMMIGRATION OFFICE, Wu Ying prayed silently. His petitions focused on his friends more than on his own predicament.

Eventually, the office door opened and a police officer wheeled out Christian, who was now wearing a bracelet above his ankle.

Wu Ying gawked. They'd put an ankle monitor on this gentle, disabled man?

Why? Did they think he would try to run away? In a wheelchair?

He glanced at Wei Min's feet. She did not have a monitor. But her hands were still in cuffs.

Was she going to be detained?

He certainly hoped not! She had been through enough – and besides, her brother depended on her for assistance.

Christian's guard glanced at Wei Min's. "Let's go."

Her officer nudged her elbow and motioned toward the door. Not understanding English or Hebrew, she rose tentatively, then walked to the exit.

Both of his friends left, but Wu Ying remained in the row of chairs with his guards.

"What is happening?" he asked.

One didn't look up from his cell phone, but the other shrugged. "You'll know soon enough."

Moments later, the Chinese Israeli exited the immigration official's office. He focused on Wu Ying.

"We have more questions for you."

Wu Ying stood and sighed. He had hoped to find a life of peace and tranquility outside China, but that did not seem to be happening. Instead, he stood under a cloud of suspicion and would probably get thrown out of the country.

On the bright side, he did not expect his captors here to

torture him. They might interrogate, detain and deport, but they would not beat and batter his body.

At least, he didn't think they would.

He entered the small office and took a seat without being asked. Then he focused a steady gaze on the immigration officer, who looked up from his notes. Those studious brown eyes focused on him for a long while.

Finally, the man straightened in his chair.

"Do you wish to remain in Israel, Mao Wu Ying?"

Until today, his answer would have been an unequivocal yes. But now, he almost wished to be anywhere other than here... or China.

"I do not want to be deported," he hedged. "There, I will certainly be imprisoned and tortured."

"Because you went absent without leave from the military?"

Wu Ying hesitated. That was only part of the reason. The other was his conversion to Christianity.

He did not know a lot about immigration law, but he knew that religious persecution was a valid reason for asylum. He could honestly be a religious refugee. But he also knew that Christianity was not welcome here in Israel.

And yet, if he failed to declare his religion and his reasonable fear of torture for that in China, he would likely be deported.

"Mister Mao?" The officer peered at him through those square glasses. "Please answer the question."

Wu Ying swallowed, then nodded.

"Yes. I would be imprisoned for that." He drew a deep breath. "And also, I would likely be tortured because I am a Christian."

8

After the meeting concluded, Ivan lingered in the ballroom. Dozens of leaders approached him with questions and suggestions. President Abramov stood beside him, and his aide hovered nearby. Finally, the crowd dwindled, and the president turned to Ivan.

"You must be tired. You've had a very long day, for your first day back on the job."

"Actually, I feel good," Ivan said, and he meant it. "I am glad to be back."

"I suspect your doctors told you to take it easy."

Ivan gazed at the older man and gave a slow nod. "They did. But I feel quite well."

"And you've abandoned your walker." President Abramov tilted his head. "You're not even using a cane?"

Ivan smiled. "It seems work is rehabilitative in itself."

"Normally I would disagree, but...." The leader eyed Ivan and shook his head. "It does appear to be the case, at least for you."

They walked toward the exit, and the president's aide fell in behind them.

"The Duma will meet formally tomorrow to consider all our military options," Abramov said. "It seems many members are leaning toward your plan."

Ivan thought so, as well, but he wasn't sure how to reply. Finally, he said, "I am sure they will make the best decision."

"Of course." The president stopped as they reached the top of the stairs.

Ivan regarded the wide, long flight of steps. Could he descend without assistance? This morning, he would have been certain it was impossible.

He reached for the railing, and felt the president's eyes studying him. Inhaling deeply, he took a step down. Then another.

President Abramov started down the stairs, continuing his conversation, but Ivan barely registered a word of it. He was walking down a flight of stairs with no issues whatsoever!

At the bottom of the stairs, they turned the corner and began descending the second flight. Ivan didn't stumble or lurch or even pause. His feet, ankles, knees and hips worked perfectly, and it felt as if he'd never spent a day in the hospital.

"Go home," the president urged. "Get some rest. Tomorrow will be a busy day."

The men parted ways at the bottom of the stairs. Ivan returned to his office, called for his car, and gathered some physical files and his laptop.

As he exited the building, his driver hurried toward him. The man's eyebrows lifted slightly, and his gaze darted around Ivan.

"Your walker, sir?"

Ivan waved him off. "No need."

The man stared for a moment before hurrying to open Ivan's door.

As he settled into the vehicle, he felt the first twinge of

fatigue. No, it was a simple tiredness... the feeling one gets after a good, hard day at work.

He fastened his seatbelt as the driver pulled away from the curb.

Marina and the children would be impressed by his recovery. No doubt they were expecting an exhausted, feeble man to return home. Instead, they'd get the old Ivan – strong and hearty and ready for a good meal. His stomach rumbled as he imagined what Marina would place on the table... perhaps his favorite, beef stroganoff.

Minutes later, his driver pulled up in front of the apartment building. Ivan exited the automobile, slung his briefcase strap over his shoulder, straightened his posture, and strode to the entrance. Inside, he took the elevator up to his floor, then made his way down the hall to their new home.

Before he could insert his key, the door flung open and Nina wrapped her arms around his waist.

"Papa! What took you so long? We were worried." She leaned back and fixed those big blue eyes on him. "Are you alright?"

"Am I late?" His gaze shifted to the clock near the door. He was an hour later than normal.

The fragrance of beef, gravy and noodles met him as Marina stepped from the kitchen, wiping her hands on her apron. Relief filled her eyes and relaxed her tense face.

He offered her an apologetic smile.

"I'm sorry, my love. I didn't realize the time."

"At least you are okay." She gave him a peck on the cheek, then glanced around him. "Where is your walker?"

"I don't need it anymore." His smile widened. "I'm getting around perfectly well without it."

"But how?" Puzzlement wrinkled her brow.

"I am on the mend." He lifted his arms. "I feel great! Except I'm famished."

"Come and eat." She took his briefcase, then eyed him again. "We have been praying for your healing, you know."

Ivan frowned momentarily, then banished the expression. He hardly believed Marina's prayers actually had any effect on his recuperation. But what good would it do to antagonize her?

Her newfound beliefs were steering her away from the vodka bottle, and she was a better mother for it. A better wife, as well.

They entered the kitchen and settled at the table.

"Where's Anton?" Ivan asked.

"He's gone to see a movie." Marina dished a plate of the stroganoff and handed it to him.

"With whom?" He picked up his napkin.

Marina shrugged. "I'm not certain. He said he was going with a group of friends."

"That's a lie," Nina exclaimed. "He went with a girl!"

IN THE COMMUNICATIONS SHACK, Sierra waited until ten minutes after seven before she rose from her chair. "I guess they're not gonna check in tonight."

Alfred began powering down his gear. "Apparently not. See you in the morning?"

"If Austin's not back by then." She paused by the door. "Aren't you going to the meeting tonight?"

"I'd better not." He glanced at her, then back at his equipment. "That mayor can get my blood boiling."

"I know, but Austin needs somebody to stand up for him.

He didn't even know about this meeting. And you're on our side, right?"

He didn't meet her gaze. "I try not to take sides."

"Oh." Sierra shot him her most disappointed look. "I guess I'll see you tomorrow, then."

She stepped out and closed the door quietly behind her.

Things would probably not go well for Austin at this meeting.

He had developed a small group of good friends on the island, but he'd only lived here a few years and he'd been a hermit until the war. The mayor, on the other hand, had been here a long time and tried to befriend everyone. People were still getting to know Austin, while everyone knew Jake Williams.

Like in most small towns, nobody who lived here wanted any more people to move into the area. Newcomers often brought strange ideas, tried to control their neighbors, and usually voted for the same ideologies that had resulted in their fleeing their previous locales due to high taxes, drugs and crime.

Besides that, Austin's family had special problems, including dementia and schizophrenia. It wasn't like they'd be ready to pitch in and work all day at the farm.

She slowly made her way to the fellowship hall, praying silently as she walked.

Several times, she glanced over her shoulder, hoping to see Austin emerge from the forest. If he made it home in the next few minutes, he wouldn't be happy to hear this meeting had been scheduled... but he'd be even less happy to learn of it tomorrow.

The room was beginning to fill up as she entered. Normally, she and Austin helped wash the dishes from dinner, but others were doing that this evening.

She scanned the crowd. Grandma wasn't here yet, and neither were McKenna and Tristan.

"Sierra!" A friendly voice drew her attention to a table near the front. Daisy waved. "Join us."

Thankful for a good friend, Sierra made her way to Daisy's table and eased into the chair across from her.

Daisy peered past her. "Where's Dustin?"

"Austin!" She corrected with a fake scowl. "He's on a hike out to his cabin site."

Daisy's back straightened. "He's not coming to the meeting?"

"I doubt he knew about it. I only found out a few minutes ago."

"Oh dear." Her lips pressed together. "That's not good."

"It's not fair, is what it's not."

"True." Daisy's brown eyes scanned the room. "Too bad he was a hermit so long. He'd have a lot more friends if he'd hung around town and gotten to know people before the war."

"Lots of people know him now. He's the new pastor!"

Daisy sighed. "Even so...."

She didn't finish her thought, but she didn't need to. Sierra could guess what she was thinking. Austin needed a lot of friends in his corner right now, and he didn't have them.

Laszlo Koval, one of the farm elders, made his way forward and stood in front of the white board. As usual, he was clad in a flannel shirt and denim overalls, looking like the epitome of a hayseed farmer.

"Can I have your attention, please?" His authoritative voice swept across the gathering crowd and silenced it.

"Thank you." He paused as his eyes searched the familiar faces. "This meeting has been requested by Mayor Williams to consider the potential influx of new residents here on the island."

He turned to the mayor, who hovered at the front corner with several members of Hideaway's erstwhile city council. "Why don't you come up and explain what you'd like to discuss?"

Jake Williams smiled as he strode to the front of the room.

"Thank you, Laszlo." He turned to the audience. "And thank you all for coming. As you may have heard, Canada is moving to evict as many as a million U.S. citizens in the coming days. Since the Lower 48 is in such dire circumstances, many of those citizens may wish to come here."

A collective gasp rose from those who apparently hadn't yet heard that news.

Sierra rubbed her arms. It *was* a dire prospect.

"I think it would behoove us all to consider this possibility, and what we might do about it," the mayor said. "As you know from local reports on the ham radio, many Alaskans are starving to death. As winter approaches, survival will become even more difficult. I suggest that we put our heads together and come up with a workable plan for our community."

AS HE EMERGED from the forest behind the farm, Austin glanced at his watch. It was nearly eight p.m. He had double-timed it back, but it had been a long, hard slog. Major panted as he trotted beside him.

At least the sun was still up. That was one of the best things about Alaska's summers – at this latitude, it didn't get dark this time of year. The sun set late and rose early, and in between, twilight ruled the wilderness.

Further north, the sun did not set for weeks in the summer – but conversely, in the winter, it failed to rise for weeks.

Austin headed straight to the ham radio shack, not really

expecting to find anyone there this late, but perhaps someone had left him a note indicating whether his relatives had radioed in that evening.

The door hung open as he approached.

Alfred Herrington looked up from sweeping the floor with a corn husk broom. "Might want to head over to the fellowship hall. There's a meeting."

"About what?" Austin's shirt clung to his damp back. He would need a bath before he'd be presentable.

"The mayor called it. About newcomers to the island."

"You mean my family?" Austin clenched his jaw. "He called a meeting while I was gone?"

"I reckon." Mr. Herrington turned to look at the four clocks on the wall. One displayed Alaska time, while the others represented the time zones of Tokyo, New York and London. "It was supposed to start half an hour ago.

Austin wiped his damp brow on his sleeve. "Did my family check in tonight?"

"Nope. But your girlfriend came by and waited to see if they would."

His girlfriend? That was the first time he'd heard Sierra called that. Of course, they hadn't been concealing their relationship – but that made it sound so official.

Their connection was important and meaningful, but he and Sierra hadn't attached any labels to it yet. It had simply blossomed over the summer, like the fragrant wild roses that bloomed all over Alaska.

"Uh, okay." Austin swatted a mosquito on his arm. "I guess I'll go see what's happening at the fellowship hall. You coming?"

"I'd better not." The old man eyed him. "Might say something I'd regret."

Austin might do the same, but he was certainly going.

Late and sweaty and all.

AFTER INFORMING the immigration officer that he was a Christian, Wu Ying tried not to panic. He lowered his gaze, then instantly raised it again to catch the official's reaction.

The man's eyes narrowed. He turned to his computer, tapped some keys, scrolled the mouse, then turned back to Wu Ying.

"There is no mention of religion in your application for asylum."

"I know." He hung his head. "I was afraid... that I'd be rejected for that."

"Religion persecution can be a legitimate reason for asylum."

"I understand."

"Your friends listed that as their basis for refugee status."

He glanced up. "Why do you think he is in a wheelchair? His feet were broken because he would not recant his faith."

"So he said." The officer leaned back in his chair and steepled his fingers. "And yet, this is the first you've mentioned of your own faith."

Shame heated Wu Ying's face.

"I was afraid to mention it." He looked up defiantly. "It is my understanding that Christians are not particularly welcome in Israel."

The man's jaw tightened. "Israel is home to people of many faiths. And to people of no faith at all."

"Of course." He lowered his gaze. "I understand."

"Good." The immigration officer turned to his computer and fell silent for a few seconds. Then he drew a noisy breath and looked at Wu Ying.

"If you do not wish to return to China, perhaps we can come to an agreement."

"An agreement?" Wu Ying blinked. This was not expected. Generally, a person is either granted asylum or denied it. A wave of caution flooded his mind. "What sort of agreement?"

"My superiors suggested the possibility when we discovered the discrepancy in your military rank information." He rested his hands on his desk. "You were at the upper echelon in the Peoples Liberation Army. You know things. You know people."

"Yes," Wu Ying answered warily. He sensed where this might be going, and he did not like it.

Not at all.

"It is possible that we could overlook your lack of transparency on your application, and continue considering you for asylum, if you are willing to help us." He cocked his head and eyed Wu Ying. "You *would* be happy to help your new country, wouldn't you?"

"What do you have in mind?" He felt certain that he already knew what the Israeli was suggesting, but he wanted him to state it outright. He had plenty of experience with vague, cloaked words and meanings, and he was done with that.

The immigration officer leaned forward and fixed him with a stare. "We could use your expertise. You have knowledge of the top-ranking officials' plans, patterns and pretenses. You have contacts inside the military. You have information on weapons systems and strategies."

Several seconds ticked by as the two men studied each other.

"You are asking me to betray my country," Wu Ying stated flatly.

The man shrugged. "You claim to be afraid to return there.

You want to live in Israel? Why would you not want to help the country that welcomes you and offers you a new home and a new beginning?"

"My government is... oppressive, but I would not want to bring any harm to the Chinese citizenry."

"We are not at war with China," the immigration officer pointed out.

"But that could change." Wu Ying felt terribly thirsty. "Then what? The population here would consider me an enemy because I am Chinese, and I may have endangered my innocent countrymen."

"A war with China seems eminently unlikely. They are very weak. They were hammered in the nuclear exchange, and battered by the mega-tsunami. I don't think you need to worry about a conflict between China and Israel in the near future."

"Your requested assistance is not a small thing." Wu Ying frowned. "I am not familiar with immigration or asylum law, but...."

A substantial silence ensued before the immigration officer spoke.

"You can certainly decline this proposal." The man squared his shoulders. "But you should be aware that your request for refugee status is likely to be rejected."

Wu Ying's heart raced. "On what grounds?"

"Your failure to reveal your previous military rank."

"But what about my religion? Religious persecution is a valid reason for refugee status," Wu Ying implored.

"Yes, but I don't think you'll qualify for that."

"Why not?" He sucked in air.

"You failed to mention it until today." The man ran a finger under his collar. "I cannot be certain you are actually religious. Since you didn't list it on your application, and only revealed it today, when you are in fear of being deported... that's not very credible. It appears you were grasping at straws to avoid being sent back to China."

9

Ivan lifted a forkful of stroganoff, then paused and glanced at Nina. "Which girl did Anton take to the movies?"

He savored the noodles as his daughter wrinkled her face. "Sophia Galkin."

He didn't recognize the name. "You don't like her?"

Nina shook her head, sending a cascade of brown curls over her shoulder. "No, Papa. None of the girls like her. She's a snob. All of the boys like her, though."

"They do, do they?" He glanced at Marina and winked. "I wonder why that could be?"

Nina spun her fork in her noodles.

"She's pretty, I guess," she groused.

"And do you know how old she is?"

"Fourteen. But she looks really old." Nina glanced at him. "Like eighteen!"

Marina blanched.

Ivan suppressed a laugh. "Old like eighteen, you say?"

Nina nodded. "Yes. She doesn't look like a girl. She looks like... a woman. All curvy and stuff!"

This time, Ivan's laugh erupted, and Nina stared at him.

Marina intervened. "Eat your noodles, Nina Ivanova."

The girl looked baffled, and Marina gave Ivan a cautionary look. In response, he raised his eyebrows and shrugged.

His wife frowned. "I am not happy about Anton deceiving me. And I'm not pleased it is regarding another girlfriend."

"I see." Ivan set down his fork. Marina had a point. He did not want his son to become a liar, and he was not enthusiastic about the boy's choice of girlfriends – or the recent outcome of his last misadventure in love.

"I will talk to him," he said.

"Perhaps I should do it," Marina countered. "I was the one he misled, and he still seems angry at you."

"For what?"

"For everything, I guess." She shrugged. "For the death of Daria, for the loss of our home, for the war, for us being here... in Siberia."

Her lip quivered and she averted her eyes.

"He blames me for all that? Truly?" Ivan asked. "Teenagers can be irrational, but honestly... do I control everything? Am I God?"

"No," Nina piped up. "God lives in heaven."

"God doesn't exist, Nina." Ivan lowered his voice. "He's a myth."

"What?" Nina's mouth hung open. She turned to her mother. "Is that true?"

Marina shot Ivan a glare before turning to their daughter. "Your father doesn't believe in God, sweetheart. But I do, and you can, too."

Nina clamped her mouth shut. She looked from her mother to her father, then back again. Then silently, she laid her napkin on the table and slid from her chair, leaving the room without another word.

Marina turned her gaze on him. "Well done, Ivan. Very well done."

"What?" He spread his hands wide. "Just because I'm not ready to embrace your newfound religion...."

She rose and picked up her plate. "It's not only that. You're driving away your son, and confusing your daughter."

"I am not the one confusing her." He pointed his finger at Marina. "That's all on you. Everything was fine before you decided to go to the cathedral."

"Was it, Ivan?" She stared at him. "Was it fine?"

He glared back, but didn't respond.

No, their life had not been fine then, and it wasn't fine now, either.

AT THE MEETING in the fellowship hall, Sierra listened to conflicting advice and arguments on how to deal with a potential influx of new residents.

"I don't even see how they'll get here," Tom Johnson said. "It's not like we have any operational airports."

"You'll probably be happy if they do come," a woman in the back interjected. "You'd make a mint with your taxi service!"

"Only if they can pay for it," Tom muttered.

Sierra rolled her eyes. Tom always got paid. Not in cash, but in labor or food or whatever his fares could provide.

In these times, it was actually a good business model.

"Please, people. Focus." Mayor Williams raised his hands to reign in the conversation that buzzed around the room. "This is a serious problem, and deserves serious consideration."

"I don't see how we can do anything about it." Grandma's

voice rose from the back of the crowd. Sierra turned to find her sitting with Jim Jenkins and his family. "It's not like we can control who arrives here."

"Or maybe we can," the mayor suggested. "That's what this meeting is all about."

"Is it?" Austin's voice rang out. "Or is it about my family?"

Sierra whirled and spotted him in the doorway. Apparently, he'd just arrived. The door hadn't even fully closed behind him.

Tension mixed with the relief she felt as she saw him. She was so glad he'd made it in time to defend himself, but she felt terrible that he had to do so.

The mayor held out his hands in a placating manner. "It's not just about you, Austin. Or your family."

"Oh, good. Because I'd hate to think you'd called a meeting to talk about my family while I was away from the farm and couldn't attend."

A murmur rippled across the crowd.

Angry eyes turned on the mayor. Including Sierra's.

"No, no. Not at all." He shook his head and offered a flimsy smile. "Now, we learned about this million-man crisis from your family, but they aren't the specific reason I called this meeting."

"Actually, the elders called the meeting," Grandma corrected. "Not you."

"Of course." The mayor smiled. "That's absolutely correct. I only requested it. They apparently saw the value of my proposed discussion."

He turned to Austin. "However, your family members hope to come here specifically, so let's begin with them. What can they provide to the community?"

AUSTIN FELT heat rise in his face. He crossed his arms and focused on the mayor's steely blue eyes.

"That's really not your business. If hundreds of thousands of refugees are coming this way, my four relatives are the least of your concerns."

A lady in the back raised her hand. "How in the world are we going to keep all those people away from our island?"

Tom Johnson stood up. "That's what I was saying before... I don't even see how they would get here. They can't fly in. There's no roads to get here. No ferry service. I suspect this is an unlikely problem. Not something we need to worry about right now."

"I hope you're right, Tom," the mayor said. "However, Canada wants to evict them. Canada still has resources – food, fuel, everything. They can put U.S. citizens on Canadian planes and bring them to any remaining airports or landing strips. They could put them on Canadian boats and ferry them up here and dump them off at the communities that have repaired a dock or two, like Hideaway has. Then what are we going to do?"

Mayor Williams looked imploringly across the crowd. "That could really happen, folks, and very soon. We need to figure out a plan to deal with it when it does."

Austin swallowed. "What do you have in mind?"

"I'm glad you asked." The mayor nodded in his direction but didn't actually look at him. "I suggest we send them on to the next community."

A dry chuckle rose from Austin's throat. "Oh. You mean, like Texas sent a few thousand of the millions of people who illegally crossed our southern border up to New York and Chicago? How's that going to help? The Alaskan communities south of us will keep forwarding their refugees, and we'll continue passing them along further north?"

The mayor glowered. "I'm not claiming to have all the answers. All I know is, they can't stay here. They'll starve, and we'll starve with them."

A collective murmur of agreement swelled through the crowd.

Apparently sensing his moment of support, the mayor gave Austin a pointed look. "I'm sorry, but your family members will contribute to our starvation unless they bring something valuable to the table. Do they?"

Austin let a long moment of silence pass before he responded.

"That's still none of your business. They're my family, and I'll provide for them."

A few in the crowd voiced their approval of his stance.

"That's a nice idea, but how is it going to work?" The mayor narrowed his eyes. "How, exactly, would you provide for them? Do you have chickens? Cows?"

"Not that it's your business, but I have a garden and I can hunt and fish. They'll eat, they'll contribute, and we'll all be fine."

"Again, that's a fine sentiment, but what if it doesn't work out so well? What if the fish don't bite or the deer are hunted out? When winter arrives, your garden will freeze." The mayor tensed for the kill. "Besides, where will they live? You're staying in a one-room converted wood shop. You going to have four more people move in there?"

Austin swallowed. He took a breath to calm his anger. "I don't need to answer to you. You take care of your family, and I'll take care of mine."

"I'm not saying you need to answer to me, Austin. But I think the community here –" he swept his arm to indicate the crowd – "has a right to know if you can feed four more people. I mean, what if all of us brought in four extra mouths to feed?

That would swell our population on the island to five times what it is now! And we're already struggling to just feed ourselves."

As the crowd voiced some agreement, the mayor added a final zinger.

"You can be sure, with that many people on Patmosa Island, the deer and black bear will quickly be hunted to extinction. A year from now, we'll all be dead."

IN THE IMMIGRATION OFFICE, heat flooded Wu Ying's face.

"But I *am* a Christian," he insisted. "You can see from tracking my phone that I've been attending church services since I arrived in Israel."

The immigration officer gazed at him. "That's been how long... a month?"

"Approximately, yes."

"Did you attend church in China?"

"No. I was converted during the war. I'm a new believer."

"Perhaps you can see how that seems unlikely or implausible. Especially considering you never mentioned religion on your application for asylum. Then today, you bring it up." The man leaned forward and continued in a milder tone. "Look, I want to help you. But I'll need you to help us."

Wu Ying sighed. "I will need to think about your proposal."

The official eyed him.

"We can give you a little time, but not much. You will need to make a decision promptly." He leaned back in his chair. "I could detain you until you reach a decision, but I don't want to do that. I'm going to let you return to your apartment."

Wu Ying maintained steady eye contact.

"Thank you for the courtesy." He tried to minimize the irony in his tone.

"You must keep your cell phone with you at all times, and keep it charged. Follow all the requirements on the order you received when you arrived in Israel." He fixed Wu Ying with a stare. "If you break any of the rules, you will most certainly be departed to your home country. So don't."

"I won't. That would be foolish."

"And make your decision soon. This offer will not remain open for long."

"I understand."

"Good. You are free to go. An officer will transport you to your apartment."

Moments later, Wu Ying was ushered from the building and whisked away in a police cruiser, which took him directly to his home. He had missed both breakfast and lunch, but now he wasn't hungry. In fact, the thought of food made him nauseated.

He entered his apartment and locked the door behind him, then sank into his recliner.

Until today, he had been happy in Israel. He loved the weather, the ancient and modern cities, the conveniences and services and especially the clean air. The feeling of freedom lifted his spirits, and the Mediterranean Sea mesmerized him.

Now, oppression crowded around him like the enemy states that surrounded Israel.

Leaving here and going to another nation was not an option. He'd been informed that he must remain in Israel while his asylum application was pending – and if it was rejected, he would be transported back to China. Not to another nation of his choice.

So he would either live here, or return to his native country.

And to remain here, it was clear he would have to betray China.

He wasn't sure why that bothered him so much. He had no allegiance to the Chinese government now, and he despised their communist oppression.

Still, he was greatly troubled by the thought that he might reveal something that could harm his countrymen.

Perhaps Christian and Wei Min would have some wisdom to illuminate this murky minefield. He would ask them tomorrow – if they were still willing to speak with him after the trouble he had accidentally brought down on them today.

10

E arly the next morning, Ivan rushed to work, arriving at the Siberian kremlin as the sun's early rays brushed the taiga. The mighty Irtysh River swallowed the waters of the Tobol River at their confluence. Together, they lifted glistening waves toward the sun, which crowned them with sparkling diamonds. Ivan shaded his eyes from the brilliance as he strode into the building.

The State Duma, Russia's lower house of parliament, would be meeting this morning and officially considering Ivan's war plan in a closed meeting. Then this afternoon, the Duma's recommendation would be sent to the upper house, the Federation Council.

Sadly, since the destruction of Moscow, all such meetings were held here, in Tobolsk, which temporarily served as the seat of Russia's national government.

Ivan had worked late last night at home, and now felt as prepared for these meetings as he could be, given the limited time frame. A bit of nervous energy boosted his mood and sharpened his cognition.

Stepping into his office, he moved toward a small mirror

with a decorative gold frame that hung on the wall near his door. He checked his appearance, straightened an emblem on his uniform, squared his shoulders and noticed that his face did not appear pale or ashen. His color looked good today.

It reflected how he felt – strong and resilient. He'd survived the heart attack and the pneumonia, he'd learned how to walk again, and now he felt surprisingly healthy.

Marina's words about her prayers for him rang in his memory, but he brushed them aside. He'd had good doctors – some of the very best. And aside from the cardiac issue, he had good genetics. He could still expect to live a long, reasonably healthy life.

Turning abruptly from the mirror, he walked to his desk and began reviewing his notes from last night, then read his incoming email messages, then texts. He placed a few calls, and before he knew it, it was time for the Duma's meeting. Four hundred fifty members would be considering his plan. Well, perhaps a few less than that – he'd learned of the deaths of five members over the past months.

None had died as a direct impact of the war, but perhaps had succumbed to the resulting stress and grief, passing due to strokes or heart attacks in the weeks that followed.

An aide rapped on his closed door a few minutes before the meeting was scheduled to begin. Ivan rose and hurried to the ballroom, which had been set up for the closed-door session. He was seated at the front of the room, between the minister of defense and the president.

The Duma's chairman called the meeting to order, then requested a brief overview from President Abramov. This was followed by the defense minister's presentation. Ivan then provided additional information and took questions from the members.

There were several questions he was unable to answer, but

the president and minister of defense stepped in to answer those.

After two hours, the politicians seemed to have their fill of information. The chairman called a brief recess, after which the Duma would reconvene for deliberations.

President Abramov turned to Ivan and spoke quietly. "It might be helpful for you to remain for the rest of this meeting. I expect additional questions will arise."

"Of course," Ivan agreed. "I am happy to be of assistance."

Soon, the chairman called the meeting to order, and Ivan listened to the members debating his plan. From their comments, he surmised they were skeptical but generally supportive.

He was not surprised when, after two more hours, they voted to send the plan to the Federation Council.

As the meeting adjourned, his stomach growled.

President Abramov glanced his way. "Perhaps you can join me for lunch. We can discuss remaining concerns and prepare for the Council meeting together."

"Thank you." Ivan gave a nod. "That sounds like an excellent idea."

He tried to maintain a pleasant but bland expression, but inwardly, he thrilled at the prospect of a private lunch with the president. Only a month ago, President Abramov had made the decision to spare Ivan's future.

Now, he was back in the inner circle.

In fact, his prospects and status had never been better.

AUSTIN CLIMBED OUT OF BED, groggy after barely sleeping following the contentious meeting the previous evening in the fellowship hall. Nothing had been resolved, and he didn't see how it would be, either.

As he stirred a small bowl of oatmeal, it occurred to him that as a Christian, not to mention a pastor, he should be looking at this problem through a spiritual lens, not a natural one.

God had all the answers Austin needed.

He set the oatmeal on the table and sank to his knees on the rag rug Mrs. Forester had generously given him.

Bowing his head, he spoke aloud.

"I'm sorry, Lord. I should have been looking to You and setting an example for Your people and this community, but I got all wrapped up in my own concerns. I ask You to forgive me, and set me on a new path. The right one. Yours."

Then he raised his head toward Heaven and prayed for a few more minutes before returning to his formerly hot cereal.

As he tasted the bland mush, a strange noise emanated from his door. It sounded like a raccoon or something scratching the wood.

Hoping it wasn't a skunk, he opened the door an inch and peered out.

Pastor Parker's dog stuck his nose into the slight opening and pushed against the door, prying it open.

"Major. What're you doing here?" He swung the door wide. "Did you abandon your post at the parsonage?"

The Belgian Malinois darted inside, following his nose around the small living space.

"You wanted to see where I lived?" Austin gave the dog a pat. "It's not much, but it works for me."

The dog beelined for his unfinished oatmeal.

"Oh, I get it. You're hungry. Touring the neighborhood, looking for the best breakfast?"

Major whined and gave him a pleading look.

"Alright, you scoundrel. I'll eat half and let you have the rest." Austin gulped a couple more bites as the dog watched intently. "There's really not enough to share."

Major sat down and whined again. Austin took one more bite, then set the bowl on the floor.

"Fine. Knock yourself out."

The dog finished the meal in two gulps, then licked the bowl intently. Then he stretched, licked his lips, and bounded onto Austin's bed, where he circled and lay down, curling his tail over his feet like a fox.

"Well, just make yourself at home, why don't you?"

A knock sounded on his door.

Austin hurried to open it, and couldn't hide his smile when he saw Sierra. He motioned her inside.

Major raised his head and issued a single bark at the visitor.

"You adopted him?" Sierra glanced at the floor. "And you're letting him lick your dishes?"

"What can I say?' Austin shrugged. "He's a hungry boy."

She looked aghast. "Gross! You could give him a dog dish."

"I'm going to wash it...."

"Gross. That's disgusting. Not to mention, unsanitary."

He picked up the bowl.

"There you go, with all your high and mighty nurse talk about sanitation," he teased.

Her eyes sparkled as she relaxed into a smile.

Sierra eyed the black-haired, good-looking former hermit. She was lucky – no, blessed – that Austin was interested in her. He deserved better, but on this island, she didn't have too much competition.

He reached for her hand. "I've been thinking –"

His words were interrupted by an electronic beep. He dropped her hand and pulled the little radio from his belt holster as someone began talking.

"Pastor Austin? This is Alfred Herrington at the radio shack. Can you swing by here?"

Austin's gaze shot to the clock, and Sierra's heart fell. She wasn't going to get a chance to chat with him.

"Is it my family?" He turned to the small clock. "They're a bit early."

"No, no, it's not that." The ham operator cleared his throat. "It's – well, it's some bad news from the Outside."

"Alright. I'm on my way." He replaced the radio in its holster, then looked at her. "You want to come with me?"

She sighed. "Sure. Let's go see what's going on."

As she stepped to his door, Austin let out a low whistle. "Come on, Major! Let's go."

The dog leapt off the bed and was at the door before Sierra could open it.

Austin led with a brisk pace, and she kept up but didn't talk much on the way to the farm. The U.S. had been hit with so many catastrophes already.

What was left to be happening now?

Her world had been completely upended a couple of months ago. Selfishly, she hoped that whatever was happening now in the Lower 48 wouldn't have much effect on Alaska.

As they neared the parsonage, Major took off and bounded up the steps, then settled on the front porch. He seemed to still be waiting for Pastor Parker to return.

When they reached the radio shack, a small crowd had begun gathering. They made room for their new pastor, and Sierra entered with him.

Alfred glanced their way, lifting his chin in acknowledgement of their arrival. Then he spoke into his microphone. "And which ones have gone into meltdown?"

A brief moment of static came through the speakers before a man replied.

"Diablo Canyon in California began meltdown when it got hit by the mega-tsunami. Columbia Generation Station in Washington State, and Arkansas Nuclear One apparently failed this past week. It's difficult to get accurate info, of course, given the situation."

Sierra froze. Clearly, the hams were talking about nuclear plant meltdowns. It was something she hadn't even considered, but now it seemed so obvious.

With the country overrun by Chinese and Russian troops, and then the nuclear war and the tsunami, and now most of the survivors of those events were dying of disease and starvation – who was left to properly maintain those power plants?

Even if the facilities were EMP-hardened and maintained an emergency supply of food for the staff, most of the workers would eventually leave to find and protect their own family members.

Assuming the plants had been properly shut down during or after the war, there was still the problem of cooling the spent fuel rods. That could take a long time. Sierra didn't know how long... years? Decades?

Alfred exchanged a significant look with Austin before continuing his radio conversation.

"How many nuclear power plants are there?"

"I've heard that there are at least ninety reactors that were operational when the war broke out," the other man answered. "I don't know how many power plants there are. The Arkansas plant had two reactors, I think."

Alfred waited for the other man to completely finish his

transmission, then asked, "So, one facility melted down in California, and one in Washington State, and one in Arkansas... do you know where the other reactors are located?"

"It's my understanding that the vast majority are east of the Mississippi River. I know there was one in Arizona, and something planned in Idaho – but all the rest are in the Midwest, or southern states or the East Coast."

Alfred sat in silence for a moment before leaning closer to his microphone. "Is anything being done? Is there any kind of government response?"

After a long pause, the other ham answered.

"I'm not sure you understand the situation here in America. There is no government. No police, no military, no emergency response of any kind. All the power has been out since the war. There's no food, no water service. It's every man for himself, and most of them are dying like flies."

Sierra tried not to be annoyed at the man's comment about America. Alaska was America, too, although sometimes it seemed people forgot that. She'd once overheard a visitor from California asking if they could use American cash in a gift shop in Juneau.

"I guess you had your radio gear in Faraday cages when the bombs went off?" Alfred asked.

"My old backup gear, yeah. All my modern equipment was on the shelf, and it got fried."

"And you're in Montana?"

"That's right. High up on a mountain, all by my lonesome. Got solar, got wind, got a creek and a garden. Most of the fallout from the war missed my area, but I was in my root cellar for two weeks anyway. Now, I've got this meltdown radiation to worry about."

Alfred cocked his head. "You think it could reach you from Washington State?"

The man cursed. "I have no idea. Is this ever going to stop?"

IN TEL AVIV, Wu Ying rose early and dressed for an excursion. Anticipation mingled with doubt in his troubled mind. Some days ago, Christian and Wei Min had invited him to travel to Jerusalem with them to see historic sites there.

Did they still plan to go today? Would they still want Wu Ying to come with them?

He hoped there was some way he could undo the grief he'd brought into their lives yesterday. He would be willing to do almost anything to make it up to them.

After gathering a few items in a day pack, he picked up his sunglasses, keys and cell phone. He had left the phone on the charger overnight, so it was fully charged. The customs and immigration authorities had issued stern warnings about failing to carry it with him, or allowing the battery to die.

It was a convenient tracking device, both for the government and for him.

After making a stop at the bakery for delectable peace offerings for his friends, he walked down the street two blocks, then turned left and continued three blocks.

The siblings resided in a ground-level apartment that was wheelchair accessible. Wu Ying knocked on their door and waited with trepidation. Surely they would forgive him. Forgiveness was a requirement of following Christ.

Still, his shoulders grew tense and his breathing shallowed.

When no one responded to his first attempt, he knocked again.

Had they already left without him?

He could not blame them if they had.

"One moment." Wei Min's soft, muffled voice filtered through a partially open window. Soon, her footsteps approached the door.

The lock clicked, the door opened, and she appeared, dressed for a day of adventure touring in casual black pants and a t-shirt. A pink backpack hung over one shoulder, with a water bottle hanging from it. Her long black hair was half up, and sunglasses perched on her head.

Behind her, Christian's wheelchair clacked across the tile. He smiled, revealing the gaps from missing teeth, courtesy of the communists' beatings in the Beijing jail.

"You are very punctual," he said. "We are nearly ready to go."

Relief flooded Wu Ying. He held up the paper bag from the bakery. "I brought breakfast."

"We have already eaten," Wei Min said quietly. "But put it in your pack, and we'll enjoy it later."

"Alright." Wu Ying slid his backpack straps off his shoulders, then turned to his friends. "I am so sorry about what happened yesterday. I never intended to draw you both into my trouble."

Christian waved a hand. "It is nothing. You are forgiven."

"Thank you." He swallowed. "You don't know how good it feels to hear you say that."

"Perhaps it feels like it does when God says it?" Wei Min suggested.

"Yes." Wu Ying nodded. "Yes, very much like that. I am so grateful."

His gaze fell on Christian's ankle monitor. "I am truly sorry you have to wear that. It is ludicrous."

"Isn't it?" Christian lifted his foot a few inches. "It isn't particularly attractive, but I can mostly cover it with my pant leg."

"Shall we go?" Wei Min glanced at her watch. "We don't want to miss the bus."

The trio left the apartment, made their way to the bus station, and boarded the bus to Jerusalem.

Once the bus was underway, Wu Ying turned to his friends. "Did the immigration officer say anything unusual to you yesterday?"

Wei Min's dark eyes fastened on him, and wrinkles creased her forehead. "The entire situation felt unusual. Are you referring to something specific?"

"Yes." Wu Ying sighed. He lowered his voice so it was barely audible over the noise of the road and engine. "I am in a terrible quandary. The official confronted me about my recent rank in the CCP, and proposed that I provide sensitive information about China, in exchange for asylum here."

Christian's eyes widened. "And you are allowed to speak of that? To us?"

"He did not forbid it. An oversight, perhaps."

"I would imagine it was." Christian focused intently on him. "You have not given an answer yet?"

"No. I told him I would need to consider it." He sighed again. "But if I do not accept this proposal, I will most likely be deported."

"No!" Wei Min stared at him. "That cannot be true."

"I am afraid it is." Wu Ying moistened his lips and lowered his voice still further. "I would greatly appreciate your advice on this situation. It is most unexpected."

"Indeed it is." Christian drew a slow breath. "Have you prayed about it?"

"Only a little," he admitted.

"It needs much prayer," his friend admonished him.

"I agree, and I plan to do that. But I wonder if either of you have any initial input?"

Wei Min crossed her arms. "It may come from some resentment on my part, but I think you should reveal everything you can about the communist leaders. They are doing the devil's work."

Wu Ying pressed his lips together. He could not argue with her logic. Turning to Christian, he asked, "What is your impression?"

His friend was silent for a long moment. Finally, he turned his gaze fully on Wu Ying.

"My sister is correct in her summary of the evils of communism. Still, this is a matter which only the Lord can answer. Ask Him to guide you."

11

After a hearty and cordial lunch with President Abramov, Ivan returned to the third floor for the Federation Council's session. The Duma had advanced Ivan's plan to the upper parliamentary chamber with a qualified recommendation. Ivan entertained mixed feelings about the outcome of today's hearings – on the one hand, he certainly wanted his brainchild to be honored and selected. But on the other hand, if the federation acted on Ivan's plan and failed to secure Israel, Ivan's future would be dismal.

And perhaps short, as well.

As he took his seat to the left of the podium, he momentarily hoped the Council would find flaws in his plan, and consider reclaiming Alaska instead.

That option had been his first choice, after all. Russia would be all but assured of success in that venture. It would be like taking candy from a baby.

However, it would not be as glorious a victory, nor would it set Russia firmly at the pinnacle of world power. Only conquering the Israeli gazelle and bringing peace to the

Middle East would accomplish those objectives. The Jewish nation held immeasurable wealth, and Russia could exploit it for decades.

When Ivan was called to make his presentation, he put his heart into it. He made the military points and arguments, but then he closed with a patriotic plea.

"This is Russia's moment. If we were to live for three lifetimes, we would be unlikely to encounter another opportunity of this magnitude. When we are successful in the Middle East, Russia's future will be assured for many generations. My children – and yours – will have peace and plenty, as will their children and their children's children."

He paused and made eye contact with the most influential senators. "But we must strike now. The current global instability is in our favor, but we all know that is transitory. If we fail to take a leadership role now, we'll be forced to deal with whichever country steps into the vacuum of power."

Ivan drew a breath. "One nation will indubitably take advantage of this moment. One nation with vision will make a bold and swift move. One nation will take the reins of world leadership."

He let that sink in before firing his final shot. "I hope, senators, that nation will be our nation. It is time for Russia to regain her former glory. It is time for Russia to lead the world!"

Applause started at the back of the room, and swept toward the front.

President Abramov smiled. He stood and applauded.

A moment later, every senator rose to their feet. Applause thundered through the room, and through Ivan's heart.

The president had led a standing ovation for him!

He wished Marina could be here to witness his great

triumph. He would, of course, describe it to her later, but that would not be the same as experiencing the actual moment.

The room roared until Ivan lifted his hand for silence. As the applause died back, he glanced at President Abramov, gave him a deferential nod, then returned to his seat.

Soon, the Federation Council would make a decision. Ivan had little doubt regarding the outcome of that vote.

He only hoped that the outcome of his war would be as definitive and glorious for Russia as the image he had verbally painted for this audience.

For the duration of the Council's deliberations, he remained at President Abramov's side to answer questions. And there were a great many questions. Far more than from the Duma.

But finally, a motion was put forward, then seconded, and the matter went to a vote.

Ivan folded his hands in his lap and tried to maintain a neutral expression as the vote was taken, then tallied.

At long last, the Council speaker took her place at the podium.

"Senators, thank you for your diligence and patience today. This has been an exceptionally long meeting on a very consequential matter."

She glanced at Ivan before continuing. "The vote has been counted, and has fallen in favor of a coalition of allies advancing on Israel. The 'ayes' tallied ninety-eight votes. The 'nays' tallied eighty votes. With that, our session is adjourned."

She tapped her gavel to end the meeting, and Ivan leaned back in his chair.

The final vote had been closer than he had expected. He had won a solid majority, yes, but there had been a lot of holdouts.

Perhaps those senators were the ones who did not wish to be blamed if his gambit failed. That was understandable.

"Congratulations, Ivan." President Abramov extended his hand, jolting Ivan from his thoughts.

He rose to his feet and shook the leader's hand. "Thank you, sir. I appreciate your confidence."

The man leaned close to his ear. "There have been moments when I have questioned your impulses, but I have never doubted your patriotism."

President Abramov took a small step back before continuing. "This plan is brilliant, and if we can get our allies on board swiftly, I'm confident we will prevail."

Ivan smiled. "Yes, sir. I'm sure we will."

Actually, he was not fully convinced. Some doubts still nagged his mind.

But he had set an invasion in motion, and now he must do everything in his power to ensure its success. Including feigning absolute confidence in the victorious outcome.

AS THE HAM radio conversation came to an end, Austin tried not to think about what was going to happen to the Lower 48. It was too horrific. But everyone gathered in the little shack was talking about it.

"They're all going to blow." Larry Evan's wife, Lynnette, shook her bony finger. "Mark my words, every last one of those nuclear reactors is going to melt down!"

Sierra gasped. She turned to Austin as if looking for a denial. But he couldn't deny it. He didn't know what would happen.

"Won't other countries do something?" Sierra asked. "Come in and make sure the reactors are shut down properly?

Make sure the spent fuel rods are cooled? It's in everyone's interest to make sure they don't melt down."

Daisy gave her a kind look. "I doubt it, honey. Nobody's going to volunteer for that. It'd be a death sentence. Besides, how would they get there? How would they fend off the starving hordes?"

As much as he disliked her analysis, Austin had to agree with Daisy. She was right. Nobody was going to come to the rescue.

"What about Canada? Mexico?" Sierra turned to her neighbors. "They're going to get hit with this, if they don't do something. What about that international agency – the International Atomic Energy Agency, or whatever they're called?"

Austin rubbed his chin. She had a point.

All the other nations could sit back and shake their heads, but Canada and Mexico would get some of the radiation from ongoing meltdowns. Perhaps the worst of it would hit areas east of the reactors, but when the wind shifted north or south, the neighboring nations would get a blast of it. From now until the Lord came back.

Maybe the IAEA would come in – but they'd need to arrive with an army to fend off the starving local citizens, and to import food and fuel for their staff. Last he checked, they didn't have an army. Or a sufficiently large staff to take over operations at ninety reactors.

Jim Jenkins rubbed his white beard. "I wonder how long it takes a reactor to finish melting down. Years? Decades?"

"What?" Sierra blinked. "Are you serious?"

"Dead serious. There've been a lot of nuclear reactor incidents in my lifetime, but three big ones stand out. Three Mile Island, Chernobyl and Fukushima. Three Mile was only a partial meltdown, but it took almost fifteen years to clean up.

And that was with a functional society and everything else up and running normally."

He frowned, then continued. "Chernobyl released radiation that affected nearly all of Europe before the plant was encased in a giant concrete sarcophagus. And more than a decade later, that had to be covered again with a better containment cover."

Jim looked around at the group gathered in the communications shack. "I'm sure you're all old enough to remember Fukushima. Japan got hit with a massive earthquake, followed by a tsunami. Sound familiar? Anyway, the meltdown resulted in radioactive leaks into the Pacific for years. Cesium-137 was measured in the air across the Pacific, through the United States to the East Coast and beyond. More than a decade later, Japan was intentionally releasing irradiated water into the ocean."

Austin nodded and crossed his arms. "And that was one power plant, in a fully functional society that responded immediately to the crisis."

His gaze shifted to Sierra. Her face had paled. She wrapped her arms around herself and pursed her lips.

She wasn't taking this well.

And who could blame her?

If their country wasn't permanently devastated before, it was now. Or it would be, in the days and weeks ahead.

As Sierra reeled from the conversation swirling in the radio shack, a figure slipped through the doorway. McKenna darted through the crowded room and gripped Sierra's arm. She leaned close to whisper in her ear.

"Can we talk?"

Sierra blinked and focused on her tense face. "Yeah, of course."

McKenna pulled her through the crowd and out the door. Once outside, she maneuvered her away from the building. Then she turned her huge blue eyes on Sierra.

"I talked to Tristan. Last night."

"So that's why you missed the meeting." Sierra tried to push all other problems from her mind. "How did it go?"

"Terrible!" McKenna's eyes reddened and glistened. "He's so upset, Sierra! And worried."

"He's scared. He'll be okay."

"He left early this morning, without telling me where he was going." Her eyes widened but couldn't contain the tears. "Have you seen him?"

"No." Sierra took McKenna's hands in her own. "Was he mad? Did you have a fight?"

"I was still asleep when he left. We didn't fight. I woke up, and he was gone."

"Maybe he went to talk to his parents."

More tears leaked as McKenna shook her head. "I walked over there. They haven't seen him."

"You probably already checked the barn and greenhouses?"

The newlywed nodded and wiped tears off her face. "Yeah."

"Does he have a place where he likes to go to think?"

"No...." After her voice trailed off, McKenna said, "He goes fishing."

Sierra forced a smile that she hoped was reassuring. "Okay, there you go. That's probably where he is."

Her cousin ran a shaky hand through her long blonde hair.

"Maybe." She met Sierra's gaze for a moment. "I'm worried about him. He's been so stressed lately."

A strangled sob slipped from her throat. "The other day, he said that if he'd known all this was going to happen, he would have called off our wedding."

"What?" Sierra tried to contain her shock. "I'm sure he didn't mean that. You guys love each other."

McKenna coughed and nodded. "I think he meant he would have postponed it. Until things are normal again."

Sierra looked away. Things were *never* going to be normal again.

They were getting worse and worse with each passing day.

She pulled her cousin into a hug. "Tristan will come back soon, and he'll be okay. He's shaken right now, but he's strong. He'll pull it together."

Sierra could only imagine how he must be feeling at the thought of becoming a father in a time of such crisis.

A Bible verse about the end times flitted into her mind, but she kept it to herself. It was the one in Matthew 24 that said, "But woe to those who are pregnant and to those who are nursing babies in those days."

As the bus rolled into Jerusalem, Wu Ying felt anticipation blossom in his spirit. He and his friends planned to spend most of the day at the Church of the Holy Sepulcher, which housed both the location of the crucifixion and the tomb where Jesus was laid.

He could hardly believe he was here – in fact, if someone had told him three months ago that he would become a Christian and travel to the Holy Land this summer, Wu Ying would have laughed in their face.

What had been preposterous then was precious now.

Beside him, Wei Min and her brother gazed steadily out the window.

"Would you look at that," she breathed, pointing to the Dome of the Rock. The golden-colored Islamic dome glistened in the morning sun. "What a travesty."

The Muslim shrine and the Al-Aqsa Mosque dominated Temple Mount, leaving the Jews only the Western Wall, a retaining wall of the ancient Jewish temple that was destroyed in 70 A.D.

Wu Ying glanced at Christian. "Do you think the Jews will ever rebuild the temple?"

"Perhaps." He shrugged. "It seems unlikely today, but who knows what might transpire tomorrow?"

Wei Min removed her sunglasses. "I believe they will. The Bible seems to indicate that a temple will be here during the great tribulation, and I've heard there are some very well-funded groups preparing for the right moment to construct it."

Wu Ying pursed his lips. "The Islamic world would go crazy if the Jews damaged their shrine and mosque. Can you imagine the rage? The violence that would ensue? It would start a war."

Christian nodded. "Yes. But stranger things have come to pass. For example, can you imagine that a race of people who were displaced from their land and dispersed across the continents would retain their culture and come back together in their homeland nineteen hundred years later?"

"I can only imagine it because it did happen. One time," Wu Ying said.

"Exactly. The future Jewish return to Israel was prophesied in the Old Testament, and then the Jews were driven out in the First Century A.D. It wasn't until the Twentieth Century that they were able to return from all over the world and re-establish a Jewish state in the land that God had given their ancestors thousands of years ago."

Christian paused, then added, "To my mind, that fulfillment of prophecy is far more remarkable than any future rebuilding of the Jewish temple. Although it does seem almost impossible at this moment in time."

Wu Ying turned and gazed out the window. The Dome of the Rock cast a spell on him. It seemed at once beautiful and evil.

Much like the devil himself.

Minutes later, the bus began making its regular stops in the Old City.

Wu Ying and his friends disembarked near the Church of the Holy Sepulcher. As his feet touched the ground, electricity sizzled through his body.

Stunned, he turned to his friends.

Wei Min was assisting Christian off the wheelchair ramp. They did not appear to notice anything unusual.

"Did you feel that?" Wu Ying stared at them.

Christian wheeled his chair away from the bus.

"I did not feel anything." He looked up. "What did you feel?"

"Electricity!" Wu Ying lifted his hands. "My arms are still tingling."

He turned to Wei Min. "Surely you felt it."

"No." She gave him a puzzled look. "I didn't feel a thing."

"It started in my feet, and ran up my body!"

People began looking at him, and he lowered his voice. "It happened the moment I stepped off the bus."

"Are you still feeling it?" Christian asked.

"No. It's gone now."

Christian tilted his head and smiled. "I think I know what happened."

"What? Tell me."

"We are at the place where Christ died and rose again. This is holy ground. Your body reacted to what your spirit sensed."

Wu Ying stood, rooted to the ground. "If true, that is amazing."

"How do you feel now?" Wei Min asked.

"Good. Very good." A slow grin overtook his face. "I feel great, but a little bit woozy."

A broad smile revealed the gaps of Christian's missing teeth. "That is wonderful, my friend. Very wonderful! The Holy Spirit touched you."

12

For Ivan, the days that followed the Russian Federation's decision to invade Israel flew by in a blur. International alliances were solidified, logistics were considered, provisions were shipped, and soldiers were conscripted. Six days a week, Ivan worked from dawn until dark, then slept fitfully and rushed back to work the following morning.

On Sundays, he worked from home in the morning, while Marina took the children to church. The apartment was reasonably quiet while they were away. After lunch, he often took the family to a park to enjoy the brief Siberian summer.

Anton seemed to grow more morose, but Ivan attributed this to teenaged angst. Nina had made three new friends, and seemed to be adjusting to the Orlov family's new life.

The plan to attack Israel was not openly broadcast, of course, but Ivan had told Marina that he had presented a creative military plan to the government, and it had been very well received and it was progressing day by day. Soon, it became clear to international observers that Russia was focusing military preparations on the Middle East.

One Sunday afternoon, as Nina swung on the park swings and Anton flirted with a group of girls, Marina took Ivan's hand. They walked a path that wound through the park, enjoying the pleasant weather.

"How are you feeling, Ivan?" She turned her big blue eyes on him.

"I feel good." He gave her a puzzled look. "Why do you ask?"

"You have been working so hard. Such long hours. And your doctor said –"

"My doctor was wrong about many things, my love. How long I would need assistance to walk, how much energy I would have... and yes, my ability to work."

"Still, I worry for you."

He squeezed her hand. "You needn't worry. Besides, you prayed for a miraculous recovery, did you not?"

Her face brightened. "Yes, that is right."

Ivan felt hypocritical for encouraging her foolish faith, but it lifted her spirits, so what harm would it do?

"Then do not worry about my health. It is good."

"I am glad you think so," she hedged. "And there is another matter, Ivan."

He steeled himself. "Yes? What is it?"

"Obviously, our country is preparing for war again. So soon, after we have lost so much. I fear it will not go well."

A memory of her prescient dream about nuclear weapons falling on Moscow haunted him, but he tried to dismiss it. Everyone had dreams. Perhaps one in a million came true.

"Do not worry, my love. If war begins, Russia will be well prepared. We have many allies."

"That concerns me, as well." Tension knit her brows. "Alliances with foreigners are not always secure. I wish Russia would focus on rebuilding here at home."

Her gaze turned to their son, who was chatting with a pretty girl. "I hate to see our young men going off to fight and die."

"You need not worry about Anton," Ivan said. "He is too young to be conscripted."

"He is now, yes. But many wars go on for years. Soon, he will be old enough."

Ivan sighed. "You worry too much, Marina. Nothing will happen to Anton."

"I hope you are right." She looked at him. "And I hope nothing will happen to you, my love. We nearly lost you the last time."

"Yet, here I am." He stopped walking, then pulled her close, inhaling her faint perfume. "I will always be here for you."

Doubt clouded her eyes, but she managed a weak smile. "I hope so, Ivan. I truly hope so."

Austin had always loved Sundays, but now they brought stress. Being a pastor stretched him to his limits. As he combed his hair in front of the mirror in the men's room, he prayed for the Lord's guidance in his sermon. He wasn't excited about the topic, but it was the one he felt God had laid on his heart for today.

The first strains of piano music upstairs were his cue to head up to the chapel.

For years, he had really enjoyed modern Christian music, but recently, the old hymns had taken hold of his heart. Their theology ran deep and sound. Perhaps that was because many of those songs had sprung from times of trial and grief. In any case, the elders here at Fellowship Farm leaned toward the classics that had stood the test of time, and now he appreciated that.

Hurrying upstairs, he greeted friends and neighbors, then made his way to a seat near the front of the chapel.

Soon, Bonnie Chappelle went forward to lead the worship. Her clear alto voice swept the assembly into lofty spiritual places.

Austin prayed as he sang, pleading for the Holy Spirit's anointing to be on him when he stood before the congregation. Preaching was not something he had ever aspired to, and now that it fell to him, he did not want to do it on his own.

Too soon, the music ended, and Laszlo Koval rose to lead the group in prayer. Then Austin gripped his Bible and took the pulpit.

"Please turn with me to Revelation chapter 18. We'll begin with verse 21 and continue to the end of the chapter."

As he waited for the congregation to open their Bibles and find the passage, he said, "For years, these verses have troubled me. I had a hard time imagining how this could take place. But now, after the mega-tsunami and war, and with the nuclear meltdowns beginning to occur across the United States, it seems fathomable. Not only for a single city, but for an entire region or country."

He began to read the scripture.

"Then a mighty angel took up a stone like a great millstone and threw it into the sea, saying, 'Thus with violence the great city Babylon shall be thrown down, and shall not be found anymore.'"

He stopped for a moment and explained, "I should clarify that the historic city of Babylon was destroyed about six hundred years before this was written, and it was never rebuilt. This passage is John's revelation of end times events, pertaining to the mysterious Babylon that will be totally destroyed before the Lord returns."

Austin looked down at the page. "Let's continue with verse 22, which had puzzled me so much."

Taking a deep breath, he read, "'The sound of harpists, musicians, flutists, and trumpeters shall not be heard in you anymore. No craftsman of any craft shall be found in you anymore, and the sound of a millstone shall not be heard in you anymore.'"

He looked at the congregation. "Folks, this is talking about a place that is totally wiped out. There's no music, there's apparently nobody building anything or even grinding grain for flour to make bread. This place is utterly devastated. We'll come back to this in a few minutes."

Austin took a sip of water that one of the elder's wives had kindly set near the pulpit for him. Then he continued on to the next verses.

"'The light of a lamp shall not shine in you anymore, and the voice of bridegroom and bride shall not be heard in you anymore. For your merchants were the great men of the earth, for by your sorcery all the nations were deceived.

"'And in her was found the blood of prophets and saints, and of all who were slain on the earth.'"

AS THE SERMON WOUND DOWN, Sierra sat in a pew beside McKenna and Tristan, listening intently. The usually quiet new pastor taught like a man on fire, bringing the scripture to life and scaring the wits out of her. In a good and godly way.

She glanced at her cousin and Tristan. Some weeks had passed since McKenna had revealed she was late. Still, her period had not come. Tristan seemed to waver between happy and scared about his wife's pregnancy.

McKenna, for her part, was glowing.

Sierra's gaze fell back to her open Bible on her lap. Austin was teaching from a terrifying passage, but she found herself especially bothered by that part about no bride or bridegroom's voices. People wouldn't be getting married?

What about her? Would she get married? She looked up at Austin just in time to see his gaze fall on her.

He was wrapping up the sermon, and announcing the baptism service.

"We have three members who have given their lives to Christ and wish to make a public profession of faith and be baptized. Sierra Forrester, Adam Baker and Jewel Kavanaugh will be baptized immediately after the service today. I hope you'll all join us in the cow pasture."

A wave of laughter rippled through the crowd.

McKenna leaned close to Sierra. "You could have been baptized in a bathtub, you know. Margie Mulligan has a real nice garden tub."

"I don't want to be baptized in a bathroom!" Sierra whispered. "Besides, only a handful of witnesses could be there. I want my whole community around me."

After the final hymn, Sierra joined the throng walking from the chapel to the pasture. The Lord had blessed the baptism day with sunshine and warm air. Grandma and Daisy carried big, fluffy towels. She'd taken Grandma's advice to wear dark, loose clothing, and she noticed that Jewel, Austin and Adam were all wearing black or navy blue clothes.

Austin took his place on the far side of the water trough as the congregants gathered around. Jewel was baptized first, followed by Adam. Then it was Sierra's turn.

She stepped into the cool water, then turned expectantly toward Austin.

"Sierra Forrester, do you believe that Jesus Christ died for your sins and rose from the dead?"

She nodded. "Yes."

"And you have received him as your Lord and Savior?"

"I have."

"Today, do you wish to make a public pronouncement of your faith, and be baptized?"

Sierra couldn't contain the smile that overtook her face as she turned and looked at her friends and longtime neighbors. "Yes. I'm a believer. A follower of Christ!"

Her announcement was met with a chorus of "Praise the Lord!" and "Hallelujah!"

Austin moved closer and put his left hand behind her shoulders. "Sierra, I baptize you in the name of the Father, the Son, and the Holy Spirit."

She pinched her nose and closed her eyes as he gripped her arm and lowered her backward into the trough.

As water swirled over her body and face, she felt like her sins were covered and washed away. Austin brought her back to the surface and she sputtered, then blinked at him.

She was not sure she had ever seen him look happier.

Grandma swooped in with a huge towel. She dabbed her own eyes with it before she wrapped it around Sierra and helped her step out of the trough.

Daisy grinned and wrapped her arms around Sierra's dripping body. "You're a new creature. Old things have passed away, behold, all things have become new. You have new life in Christ."

Moments later, she was mobbed and embraced by her friends, just as Adam and Jewel had been when they'd emerged from the water.

Eventually the crowd thinned as people headed off to have lunch.

Austin remained. He gazed at her with those happy brown eyes.

She grinned at him. "I feel so good!"

He smiled. "Of course. That's part of the deal."

"Thank you, Austin." She meant to thank him for baptizing her, but her words weren't working too well at this moment.

"You're welcome." He wrapped an arm around her and they started toward the fellowship hall. Then he stopped and pulled a piece of hay out of her dripping hair. "You've never been more beautiful than you are right now."

"With my makeup running? I look like a drowned rat."

"Doesn't matter. It's an inner beauty. A life offered to Christ."

AFTER THE SUNDAY church service in Tel Aviv, Wu Ying hosted Christian and Wei Min in his tiny apartment for lunch. As he brought the fried rice to the table, he looked at his friends.

"I've made a decision. About the proposal from the immigration authorities."

Both of them looked expectantly at him.

"Do tell," Wei Min urged.

"After much prayer, I have decided to provide my assistance. Israel is my home now, and China is ruled by demonic, wicked people." He took his seat. "Christian, would you ask a blessing on our food?"

Christian nodded and prayed, then looked at him. "Did you wish to discuss it?"

"I have made up my mind. But of course, if either of you wish to comment, I am happy to hear your thoughts."

Wei Min picked up her chopsticks. "I believe you have made the right choice."

"Thank you." He turned to Christian. "Do you agree?"

"Yes." The man reached over and laid a thin hand on Wu Ying's. "It may prove difficult, but I think your decision is correct."

"I am not happy with it, but I am at peace." He sighed. "And I am relieved that you both agree it is the right thing to do."

"Have you contacted the immigration office?" Wei Min asked.

"Not yet. But I intend to, first thing tomorrow."

He was not looking forward to that, but he could not delay it any longer. The immigration officer had made it clear he would need to make a decision in a timely fashion. Wu Ying suspected he was nearing the end of that time frame.

His heart grew heavy as he chewed his rice.

How he wished he had not been put in this position!

Still, perhaps God had placed him here in the Holy Land for this exact reason. Who could know the mind of the Lord?

He had been reading the book of Esther this week, and was touched by the passage in chapter four, where Esther feared for her life when she was requested to help save her people.

Wu Ying had committed the fourteenth verse to memory, and now he savored Mordecai's words:

"For if you remain completely silent at this time, relief and deliverance will arise for the Jews from another place, but you and your father's house will perish. Yet who knows whether you have come to the kingdom for such a time as this?"

As for himself, Wu Ying did not imagine he would provide any great service to the nation of Israel.

But who knew?

Perhaps he could provide some small benefit to his new country.

13

I t did not take as long as Ivan had anticipated to form military alliances and prepare for war. It seemed the stars aligned to make the preparations swift and sure. Infrastructure crews repaired the war-damaged roads, essential railways and aircraft runways in record time, and the military used them to move men and materiel for the invasion. Russian troops flew to Syria and Egypt, where they trained in the local terrain.

What Ivan expected to take months took only weeks.

Soon, Russia and her allies would launch their attack on Israel – and with America out of the way, there would be no one to save her.

When the war ended, Russia would become fabulously wealthy from plundering that little country.

Ivan took a sip of tea and gazed out his office window at the sparkling river. He only had a few projects to wrap up before he headed for home. From his perspective, the military could proceed to war as soon as next week.

He realized, of course, that Israel almost certainly possessed nuclear weapons. For decades, the gazelle had been vague and opaque about her capabilities in that regard. However, it was strongly believed she did have nukes, either supplied by her ally, the United States, or built by the Israelis themselves.

But would they work? Had they ever been tested? How old were they? How many devices did the Jews actually have?

There were few answers to these questions.

However, Ivan did not worry too much about Israel's nuclear status.

If Israel used any nuclear warheads against Russia, she would be totally annihilated by Russia's response. A handful of Russian nukes would suffice to wipe Tel Aviv and Jerusalem off the map – so he believed Israel would never use nukes against a nuclear-armed country. The Jews lived in a tiny sliver of land, and there was no place for them to escape nuclear radiation. It wasn't as if they possessed twelve time zones of earth's surface, as Russia did.

There would be no place for the Israelis to run and hide. All of their neighboring countries were either hostile or declared enemies of the Jews.

No, Israel would only utilize nuclear weapons against regional enemies who were not similarly equipped. Never against Russia or another nuclear power.

Nuclear devastation was one thing Russia would not have to worry about, this time around. And so Ivan did not worry about that.

He set down his tea cup, reviewed the latest reports from his subordinates, then placed a few phone calls.

When he finally hung up the phone and reached for his hat, fatigue settled over him. He'd been working hard for weeks, and it was finally catching up to him. This weekend, he would need to get some rest.

His mind and body needed a day or two to recuperate,

before the war began. Because once it started, he would have to be one hundred percent mentally and intellectually capable. He would need to be rested and energized, ready and able to work very long days with few breaks, for weeks on end.

Because this war would be conventional, rather than nuclear, it might last for a while. The Israelis would certainly hit back hard, but eventually, they'd be overrun.

Ivan estimated it could take several weeks, but with war, one could never be sure. Perhaps it would be days. Perhaps months.

He left his office and started down the hall.

Certainly, this war would not last years. Israel had no remaining friends, no allies to supply her with munitions and money.

All on her own, she would not stand long in the face of Russia's onslaught.

FOR A FEW WEEKS, Austin had heard brief updates from his cousins as they slowly made their way west, toward the Pacific coast. Canadian fuel shortages developed in the western provinces as shipments from the Atlantic were reduced, which, coupled with challenges in bartering and currency exchange, made the family's travel painstakingly slow.

Each morning and evening, Austin arrived at the communications building a few minutes before 7 o'clock, so he'd be there if they checked in.

This evening, Sierra accompanied him.

Alfred looked up as they entered the building. He mumbled a greeting, then turned back to his equipment and fiddled with some dials.

Austin eased into a chair, but Sierra remained standing. She gazed at a calendar hanging on the wall.

"Didn't your cousin say Americans had thirty days to leave Canada?" She glanced at him. "When was that?"

"I'm not sure. It must have been close to a month ago."

Alfred swiveled his chair to look at Austin. "It's strange I haven't heard much about that from other hams."

"Maybe the news hasn't really gotten out," he replied. "There's a lot bigger stuff going on."

"You can say that again," Alfred agreed. "I'm getting reports from the Middle East – it sounds like Russia is gearing up for war against Israel."

Austin swallowed. "The first Gog-Magog war. It won't go well for the Russians."

"Why not?" Sierra asked.

"It's in the thirty-eighth chapter of Ezekiel. God is going to fight for the Jews. And He's going to win, obviously."

Alfred inhaled a noisy breath. "That may be, but it's not looking too good for Israel right now. There's a whole constellation of enemies gathering at her borders."

Austin tilted his head. "A constellation?"

Alfred spread his arms wide. "Vast numbers of troops, like the stars in the sky."

"Oh."

Alfred pulled on his headphones and turned back to his radio. Austin fell silent, and Sierra came and sat down beside him. She slid her hand into his.

Suddenly, Alfred came to life. He spoke animatedly, then removed the headphones and pulled their plug, sending the audio to the speakers where Austin could hear the transmissions.

Moments later, Rick's voice came over the airwaves.

"Hey, Austin, can you hear me?"

Austin scooted close to the microphone. "Yes. I'm here. Go ahead."

"It's good to hear your voice. We should be arriving in Prince Rupert tomorrow. Canadian authorities announced this morning that they'll provide transport to regional Alaskan destinations, including all of the Inside Passage."

Austin's gut tightened. That was good for his family, but terrible for most Alaskans. He wasn't sure what to say.

"Austin?" Rick's voice scratched across the airwaves. "You hear that?"

"Yes." He cleared his throat. "Yeah. So what's the plan? Is there some kind of transportation schedule?"

"Don't know yet. We'll contact authorities when we arrive in town."

Austin swallowed. "Okay. Don't expect there to be much 'town' left at Prince Rupert. The tsunami scrubbed the coastal areas clean."

"Yeah, we're starting to see that already. I expect it'll be worse as we descend to the coast tomorrow."

"Alright. Hopefully you can find a ham operating down there."

"Keep your ears on."

Austin smiled. "I will. Be safe."

As they left the radio shack, Sierra squeezed Austin's hand. "Sounds like your family will be here soon."

"Yeah. About that...." Austin stopped and looked into her eyes. "We should talk."

He guided her toward a bench outside the recreation hall, and they sat down.

"What's up?" She couldn't keep the tension out of her voice when she saw stress all over his face.

"A few weeks ago, I asked Alfred to try to contact my dad. He didn't have any luck for a while, but last night, he got through to a ham in Bolivia who knows my dad. I was able to talk to him."

She met his gaze. "Your dad? Or the ham?"

"My dad. Both," he clarified. "Anyway, Dad had heard about the issues with displaced Americans in Canada. I told him about Grandpa still being alive, and he cried."

"Oh!" Emotion welled up in her eyes. "He didn't know his father was alive?"

"No. Personal communications have been such a nightmare in North America. Obviously." Austin took a deep breath before he continued. "So he offered to host my cousins and Grandpa."

She blinked. "He can house that many people?"

"He's got a four bedroom house, and a guest house."

"Nice!" She smiled, but Austin didn't look happy. "Why didn't you tell Rick just now? That solves all the problems, doesn't it? They'll have a place to live without being a burden on the islanders here – sorry to mention that, but this is great news, right?"

"Yes and no." Austin looked away. "I didn't tell Rick yet because I wanted to tell you first, and I expect I'll talk to him again tomorrow."

"That's nice, but... I don't understand the problem."

He leaned toward her. "Dad's going to need help with Grandpa. And with Louis."

"That shouldn't be too difficult. Isn't labor cheap in Bolivia?"

"He asked me to come down. Grandpa is slipping mentally and doesn't do well with strangers anymore. And Louis, well, he has some crazy cycles. Also, he doesn't speak Spanish. Hiring locals could be a recipe for disaster."

Sierra's lungs constricted. Austin was clearly considering leaving Alaska.

She looked away.

Austin fell silent.

She turned to him. "You're leaving. Aren't you?"

He avoided her gaze for a long moment.

"I'm praying about it." His voice was hoarse.

He gripped her hand and looked into her eyes. "I have a responsibility to my family, Sierra. You understand that, right?"

Tears flooded her vision.

Sure, she understood. But that didn't make her like it. Not one bit.

In the weeks after Wu Ying agreed to assist Israel with his knowledge and expertise, he settled into a regular schedule of meetings with the Military Intelligence Directorate, also known as Aman, and occasional meetings with Shin Bet and the Mossad.

At times, he felt distinctly uncomfortable with his Shin Bet and Mossad handlers, and suspected they were not so much interested in his military knowledge of China as they were in assessing whether he was personally a threat or double agent.

From his perspective, the Mossad was never to be trusted. They were too political, too powerful for the good of their own country, and nearly ungovernable. At times, they reminded him of the Chinese Communist Party or the American CIA.

Shin Bet functioned much like the American FBI, and Wu

Ying's contact there was a beautiful Jewish woman about his own age, with a brilliant mind and a sharp eye. He did not trust her in the least.

However, he was pleased with his work with Aman, and felt he was actually providing some small benefit to them. Its function was similar to the American NSA, but with a narrower scope of focus.

And how they focused!

While Wu Ying was not privy to the inner workings and secrets of Aman, he certainly noticed the intensity and tenacity with which the staff did their work. The professionalism of the corps was quite impressive.

In China, he had rarely seen such dedication to a government mission. Of course, staff in China were perhaps not as motivated by love of country, and their families certainly were not surrounded by belligerent enemies on all sides, either.

Israel was unique in that regard.

This morning, Wu Ying was scheduled to meet with his handler at Aman, so he was in good spirits.

He locked his apartment door and walked down to the car waiting at the curb. While China was not viewed as a particular threat at this time, Israel would not let her guard down in any direction. Therefore, Wu Ying's input was considered valuable.

He appreciated having something to do that was helpful and perhaps important. It was fulfilling – far more fulfilling than his previous work for the People's Liberation Army.

The driver made his way directly to a military installation on the outskirts of Tel Aviv, where they proceeded through two external checkpoints before entering the front door and undergoing more security screening.

That was another reason Wu Ying preferred working with

Aman to the Mossad or Shin Bet – he felt more comfortable around military staff. These were the men and women who were actively protecting their country from external threats, as opposed to the political activities initiated or conducted by the other two security agencies.

Aman was not going to stage any foreign political assassinations or internal coups. At least, that was his impression.

Every man and woman who worked in the Israeli military knew that their efforts could protect their own parents, spouses or children from being overrun and killed by enemy forces. Surely that was a strong motivation to do one's very best work.

Because Israel was such a small nation and under constant threat, it required all its Jewish young adults to serve in the military, with few exceptions. This, of course, provided several benefits to the country – in addition to having a fully-staffed military at all times, nearly all the Jewish adults had military training. So, when war came, any trained Jew under age 40 could be called up for service. It was a massive reserve corps.

Older adults, both men and woman, also knew how to use military-grade weapons to protect their homes and communities.

When he was finally ushered past Aman's security stations, Wu Ying was escorted to his handler's office.

Lieutenant Colonel Isaac Meir looked up from his computer screen. Even while seated, his military bearing was perfect, as was the regulation haircut of his dark brown hair. He motioned to the chair in front of his desk.

"Welcome, Mister Mao. Please have a seat."

Wu Ying sat, and the officer who had escorted him to the office waited by the door.

The lieutenant colonel adjusted his wire-rimmed glasses and studied Wu Ying.

"Tell me, in your work with the People's Liberation Army, did you ever have contact with a Russian major general by the name of..." his gaze dropped to his computer screen, then focused again on Wu Ying. "Ivan Alexandrovich Orlov?"

Wu Ying froze. Of course he had.

Major General Orlov had been one of his primary contacts during the preparatory period for Russia and China's attack on the United States. He and Orlov held similar positions in their countries' militaries.

Ivan Orlov's visage flashed into his brain, along with an instant headache. In his late 40's, the Russian's tightly-cropped brown hair framed a narrow face with a long nose that reminded Wu Ying of a horse. Orlov's pale blue eyes betrayed nothing. The man was an enigma.

"Mister Mao?" Meir's voice cut into his thoughts.

Wu Ying met the Israeli's sharp brown eyes.

"Yes," he sighed. "We were acquainted."

"I see." Meir studied him for a long moment. "Tell me about your... acquaintance."

Wu Ying pursed his lips, then swallowed. "He was my counterpart in the Russian military. Prior to the war, and before I was jailed, we communicated regarding our preparations and readiness for the attack."

He looked down at his hands. From the recent news, he understood that Russia was aggressively surrounding Israel with troops and military equipment. Although Russia and her apparent allies claimed this was only for training exercises, Wu Ying had doubts about that.

Meir glanced at the officer waiting by the door. With a look and a nod, he dismissed the man. Then he focused on Wu Ying.

"Our intelligence suggests that Major General Ivan Orlov is centrally involved in the planning of an invasion of Israel.

Do you have any reason to believe he would know that you are no longer in the PLA?"

"Yes." Wu Ying tried to hide his confusion at that question. "If he was not directly informed of my removal from my post, he certainly would have been aware of my absence during the launch and prosecution of the war. He would have begun working with another Chinese officer, instead of communicating with me."

Meir nodded, then pursed his lips. His gaze slid toward the bookshelf in the corner of his office. For a long moment he was silent.

"That's unfortunate." The man exhaled a deep breath, then turned his focus on Wu Ying. "Have you had any contact with him since your incarceration?"

"No. One day we were in communication, and the next, I was arrested. I have not had any contact with any Russians since then."

"So he might not be aware that you're no longer with the PLA? To his knowledge, you might have fallen ill or something?"

"That seems unlikely, but I suppose... perhaps." Wu Ying grew perplexed at the Israeli's line of questioning. But rather than ask directly, he decided to wait and see where this was going.

Abruptly, Meir rose from his chair. He strode to his window and stared out. Moments later, he turned back to Wu Ying.

"We were hoping to use you to gain information directly from Orlov. That may not be as likely as we had hoped. In the meantime, we will need to know everything you know about the man. One of our intelligence officers will interview you on that subject today, and then someone will drive you home."

He fixed his gaze on Wu Ying and added, "For the next month, we will need you to be immediately available at all times. We'll provide you with a hardened satellite phone, which you must keep on your person along with your cell phone. And don't leave Tel Aviv."

14

The next Saturday evening, Ivan kissed Marina goodbye. For safety reasons, she and the children were going to visit her cousin in a tiny enclave in eastern Siberia. The airport was packed, as nearly all military family members were leaving Tobolsk prior to the beginning of hostilities in the Middle East.

Tears swelled in Marina's eyes. "Be safe, my love."

"Of course. And you as well." He squeezed her hand. "This will be over soon."

"That is what you said about the last war." She pressed her purse against her ribs, and followed their children onto the airplane.

Ivan turned to leave, then hesitated. He had a few minutes to spare. Why not wait and watch their flight take off?

No. He had too much work to do. He would be catching a plane very early in the morning – although he would be traveling to Damascus, not a remote community.

President Abramov had made the decision to run the war operations from Syrian facilities, rather than Russian ones.

There was some logic to this – none of Russia's military leaders were interested in returning to the war bunker under bombed-out and irradiated Moscow, especially for a war that was expected to last much longer than a week. While Russia was in the process of building a new war command facility, it would not be ready before this autumn, at the earliest.

Additionally, the federation president had cited the benefit of being in the immediate vicinity of the political and military leaders of Russia's allies. Some decisions would be made jointly, and in-person consultations could make those interactions swifter, with more desirable outcomes. For those reasons and others, President Abramov had decided to personally travel to the region, rather than monitor the war's progress from his home country.

Of course Ivan and his colleagues had advised against this. A war zone was never safe, regardless of all the security measures the military would establish. But the president was determined to go, so additional precautions were instituted for his safety.

Ivan turned on his heel and strode out of the Tobolsk airport. His driver waited curbside, and drove him straight home.

He would finish his preparations, get packed, then try to get a good night's rest. It would likely be the last one in a while.

The allies had decided, on Ivan's suggestion, to launch the invasion on two fronts simultaneously. The northern and eastern allies, including Russia, Turkey, Iran and Syria, would invade across the Israel/Syrian border, into the Golan Heights. At the same time, Egypt and Libya would penetrate the Israel/Egyptian border, attacking south of the Gaza Strip to avoid that morass.

This dual approach would divide Israel's focus. It would also force her to split her troops, tanks and equipment between the opposite ends of her country.

There was no way the gazelle could stand up long under such a two-pronged assault in which she'd be vastly outnumbered by determined enemies.

Ivan looked forward to a swift and very satisfying victory and all the glory that would accompany it.

ON SATURDAY EVENING, Austin made his way to the communications shack alone. Sierra had been unusually quiet today, after their painful discussion about his family. Clearly, she did not want him to leave Alaska.

And he didn't want to go.

But didn't he have a responsibility to help his dad and grandfather?

He wasn't sure how he could get to Bolivia. Perhaps he could catch a ride on one of Canada's return flights from dropping Americans in Alaskan communities. They'd be disinclined to accommodate him into Canada, of course, but if he persuaded them he was only going to catch a commercial flight out of a Canadian city to Bolivia, it might work.

Hopefully, he could get there somehow, get his relatives settled in, and return to Alaska in the near future.

Returning here might be even more difficult than leaving.

In fact, it could prove impossible.

He hated that thought.

Until now, he had been thinking of eventually marrying Sierra. But he could hardly ask her to leave Alaska.

And he couldn't honestly expect to return to the island.

As he reached the door of the radio shack, he remembered the surprise of discovering – or rather, of Major's finding – his old motto at his former home site.

He'd asked God, jestingly, if that was a sign.

Perhaps it actually had been. Far more than he could have imagined.

He sighed as he entered the building.

Wearing his headset, Alfred looked up. "Good evening."

Austin nodded glumly. "'Evening."

He sat down and watched as the radio operator did his work.

If Rick had been able to find a ham in the Prince Rupert area, he should be checking in tonight. If not, then he would likely check in tomorrow. After Austin talked with him, one or both of them should contact Dad's ham operator in Bolivia.

Footsteps approached the door, and then Sierra appeared in the doorway. She entered and took a seat beside him.

He offered her a sad smile. "Thanks for coming."

"Of course." She reached for his hand and clutched it in a death grip, as if she'd never see him again if she let go.

Still wearing headphones, Alfred straightened in his chair. He unplugged his headphone cable and glanced over his shoulder at Austin.

"Your cousin is checking in."

Austin rolled his chair closer to the microphone. "Hey, Rick."

"Hey yourself."

Before his cousin could proceed with whatever news he might have, Austin wanted to present his own.

"I've reached my dad in Bolivia. He's invited you all to come down and stay with him there."

A long pause preceded Rick's response.

"Bolivia?"

"Yeah. You knew Dad was there, right?"

"Of course. Yeah. What's the situation down there?"

"The water and electricity are still working most of the time. They're landlocked, so no direct problems from the tsunami. Dad said things are pretty much normal there – they've got the political scandals and corruption that are typical of banana republics, but there's food and some medical services."

"Wow." Rick paused. "That's an unexpected offer."

"You should consider it. Grandpa – and all of you – will be better off there."

"What about you?"

"Dad invited me, as well. I'm praying about it."

"How would you get there?"

"That's the big question." Austin glanced sideways at Sierra, who bit her lip. "Transportation is nearly non-existent here in Alaska."

"Speaking of that, we did get information on Canada's transports of U.S. citizens," Rick said. "They printed fliers with locations, dates and times. Totally old-school. They have a web site, too, for those who can still access the internet."

Alfred gave Austin a significant look, and leaned toward the mic. "This is Alfred, the ham. Do those fliers list specific drop-off locations in Alaska? Is Hideaway or Patmosa Island on the list?"

"Yes and yes," Rick confirmed. "Hideaway is listed as having one functional dock, and the schedule shows weekly drop-offs there, beginning next week."

Alfred winced and moved away from the microphone.

Rick cleared his throat. "We signed up for Monday's transport."

Sierra squeezed Austin's hand. When he glanced her way, she gave him a hopeful, imploring look.

If Rick and Austin's family members were already signed up to come here, why discourage them now?

Obviously, they had a better offer in Bolivia, but selfishly, she did not want Austin to leave. It was hard to imagine life without him.

Austin swallowed, then spoke into the mic. "You might want to talk to my dad about his offer. He can fill you in on details and answer any questions."

"Yeah, we'll definitely want to do that. How do we get ahold of him?"

Alfred gave the details for contacting Austin's dad's ham operator, then backed away from the mic.

Austin drew closer to it. "If you come here, to the island, you might not be able to leave for a long time. We don't have any commercial transportation. No fuel for private transport. No medical facilities or grocery stores."

"I understand the situation," Rick said. "But we'll probably stay on the transport list for Monday. Meanwhile, we'll try to contact your dad. I'm not sure how we'd get down to South America."

"Isn't Canada still doing commercial flights?" Austin asked.

"From some of the major cities, yes. Here on the west coast, everything is a wreck. Like you told us it would be."

The conversation continued, but Sierra stopped listening.

She felt sick in her stomach. She clutched Austin's hand as if she'd lose him forever if she let go.

Over these past months, they'd grown close. Closer than she'd ever expected.

The thought of saying goodbye was almost incomprehensible.

She tried to understand his conviction that he was responsible to help his family, but wasn't he also responsible to the community, now that he was the pastor here?

How could he leave his flock?

And her?

In TEL AVIV, Wu Ying scoured the online English-language version of the Israeli newspapers. Things were not looking good – in fact, they were looking quite bad. Russia and a coalition of allies had basically set up war fronts at Israel's northeast and southern borders.

They still claimed it was for a training exercise which was set to begin tomorrow and continue for two weeks.

Wu Ying didn't believe it. And from what he could ascertain, his handlers in Israel's military security agency did not believe it, either.

He looked forward to seeing Christian and Wei Min tomorrow at church, and the siblings had invited him to lunch afterwards at their apartment.

Would the invasion begin before then?

If the exercise was officially set to begin tomorrow, that might actually be the launch of the war.

He glanced at the clock. It was now ten minutes after seven in the evening. Not too late for a brief conversation.

Wu Ying texted Christian and asked if it would be alright if he came by for a short visit. Almost instantly, his friend texted an affirmative reply.

He gathered his wallet, keys, cell phone and the military satellite phone, and hurried to his friends' small apartment.

Wei Min opened the door as he approached.

"Welcome." Her face brightened as she greeted him. "Please come in."

"I hope I am not imposing."

"Not at all. We are happy to see you."

Christian waited in the living room. He swung his wheelchair toward the entrance as Wu Ying stepped into the small space.

A joyful smile lit his face. "Welcome, my friend! Please, have a seat."

"Thank you." Wu Ying took the single chair, leaving the love seat to Wei Min.

"Would you like some tea?" Wei Min asked. "Cookies?"

"No, thank you." Actually, he would have liked both, but he did not wish to impose. "I don't expect to stay long."

Wei Min settled on the love seat and gazed expectantly at him.

"I am sure you have been watching the news," Wu Ying began.

"We do try," Christian agreed, "but our Hebrew is very weak. We have found some online sources in Chinese, but who knows how accurate they are?"

"Right." Wu Ying drew a deep breath. "The basic situation is, Russia has formed alliances with Israel's enemies, and even now, they are amassing on our borders. They claim it is for a military drill, but I do not believe it. I expect an invasion very soon. Perhaps even tonight."

Wei Min's face tightened. She looked at her brother, then back to Wu Ying. "Should we leave Israel?"

"I cannot, due to my obligations," Wu Ying pointed out. "However, if you are allowed to go elsewhere, I would recommend that. As soon as possible."

Christian met him with a steady gaze. "I would imagine the flights out of Tel Aviv and Jerusalem are full."

"That may be true," he agreed. "Many are fleeing the country this weekend."

"Israel may suffer greatly, but she will win this war," Christian said. "I will pray about it, but I already feel in my spirit that we will be safe here."

"I hope you are right, because it is a dangerous situation," Wu Ying pointed out. "Why do you think Israel will win?"

"Ezekiel prophesied this war over 2,500 years ago. In the book of Ezekiel, chapters 38 and 39, he refers to a war against Israel by a coalition of allies led, I believe, by Russia." He turned to his sister. "Would you hand me my Bible?"

She pulled it off the shelf and gave it to him.

Christian opened the book and flipped through the pages.

"In chapter 38, Ezekiel refers to a war that would take place in the latter years, in the latter days. He notes that it would occur after the Jews had returned to their land, which of course has been happening over the past eighty years. The Lord speaks of a leader referred to as Gog, the prince of Rosh, Meshech and Tubal. Many scholars believe Rosh is modern-day Russia. The Lord says in verse fifteen that Gog will come 'from your place out of the far north'."

Christian paused and looked at Wei Min and Wu Ying. "What is directly north of Israel?"

"Moscow!" Wu Ying exclaimed.

"Exactly." Christian's smile revealed the gaps from his missing teeth. "I would encourage you to read these two chapters tonight. You'll see that God will go to war on behalf of Israel, and will destroy the invaders."

Wu Ying sat transfixed.

Once again, the precise nature of the prophecies in scripture astounded him.

If not for the revelation of God, how could anyone have known thousands of years ago that all these events would occur?

And Wu Ying was alive during this astonishing time, and witnessing it all taking place!

15

On Sunday, as his plane descended for its approach to the Damascus airport, Ivan tugged at his collar. It felt as if the cabin heated ten degrees as it shed altitude in preparation for landing in Syria. Ivan had grown accustomed to Siberia's moderate summer temperatures, and was not prepared for the stifling heat of the Middle East.

In his military uniform, he was not dressed for it, either.

He took a sip of ice water, then held the frozen cubes in his mouth until they melted. It hardly helped.

Finally, the plane touched down, and heat radiated into the aircraft. He could not disembark as soon as he'd like, because President Abramov was traveling on this plane as well, and he would receive the full red-carpet treatment on the tarmac, delaying Ivan's rush to the air-conditioned SUVs waiting to transport the military entourage to their destination.

He watched from his window as the president descended the stairs, greeted the Syrian president and his lovely wife, posed for photos, and proceeded along the red carpet to his vehicle.

Finally, Ivan exited the back of the plane and hurried to the line of black SUVs that would take him and the other generals to the war bunker.

Before he entered the vehicle, he glanced skyward. Israel was certainly well aware of the foreign military buildup at her borders, and it wasn't beyond her capabilities to strike the Damascus airport. In fact, she'd carried out multiple airstrikes against both Aleppo International Airport and Damascus International Airport in the past.

If the gazelle struck now, she could wipe out the top leadership of her enemies' military and political structures.

Ivan ducked into the back seat of a waiting vehicle and felt the rush of cold air. If he were in Israel's position, he'd push that button and send the missiles to the Syrian tarmac.

A security officer closed his door, but the vehicle did not pull forward.

Ivan craned his neck. What were they waiting for?

The president's vehicle also idled on the runway.

Tension tightened Ivan's chest. It was time to get moving. They were sitting ducks out here.

He glanced toward the aircraft. No one exited. Apparently everyone had disembarked and entered one of the vehicles. So what was the delay?

Was there a mechanical issue? A traffic accident on the intended route? Surely they had alternate routes planned out, guarded and ready.

In spite of the icy air conditioning, Ivan began to sweat. He was trapped in an obvious target zone, clearly within satellite view of their enemy, and sitting here for no discernable reason whatsoever.

Finally, his SUV began to roll forward at a snail's pace.

Ivan secured his seatbelt and tried to relax.

The vehicle eased to a stop behind another SUV, while a

third one pulled up snuggly behind them.

If they were sitting ducks before, now they were pinned-down sitting ducks. If anything happened, his vehicle could not go forward or backward. The driver had not left room to escape.

Ivan cursed.

What was going on? And why were they still here?

He glanced up to the rearview mirror and noticed his driver's sunglasses angled toward him. Ivan nearly asked the man what was causing the delay, but he doubted the driver spoke Russian. And Ivan knew not a word of Arabic.

His heart sent him a warning pang. He had to calm himself before he suffered another heart attack. That was something he never wanted to experience again.

Once was enough.

ON SUNDAY MORNING, Austin waited at the communications shack, but his cousins didn't check in. Likely, they didn't have any more news since the previous evening. They might not have established contact with his dad yet.

Later that morning, he preached his sermon on the first Gog and Magog war, referenced in Ezekiel chapters 38 and 39. He made a point of explaining his belief that the war portrayed in Ezekiel was not the same as the second Gog and Magog war portrayed in Revelation chapter 20, which transpires at the end of the millennial reign of Christ.

He also noted that the war Ezekiel described would require seven months after the war to find and bury all the dead. And for seven years following that war, the Jews would burn Magog's weapons.

Although he thought it was an interesting topic, his

sermon somehow felt awkward and lackluster.

Perhaps he wasn't cut out to be a pastor after all. Maybe he was supposed to go to Bolivia to help his family.

After church, Sierra took a seat beside him at one of the tables in the fellowship hall in the chapel's daylight basement. She dipped her spoon in her vegetable soup and swirled it around, but didn't bring it to her mouth.

Daisy and her family sat across from them. Strangely, she'd skipped the tie-dye today, and had worn a red t-shirt with an American flag flying across the front. It wasn't exactly church attire, but most of the islanders had lost their wardrobes in the tsunami.

She studied Austin and Sierra for a long moment, then plunked her spoon into her bowl.

"Alright, you two, what's going on? You have a fight or something?"

"No." Austin tried to hide the defensiveness he felt.

"Austin's thinking about leaving the island," Sierra blurted.

"What?" Daisy's eyes widened as she straightened and leaned back. "Why? How?"

Before he could answer, her eyes narrowed. "It's about your family, isn't it? You don't want to deal with the mayor and his ilk, so you'll just up and leave."

"It's not like that," Austin objected. "My family needs a lot of help. My dad has offered to host them in Bolivia, and he needs my assistance."

"Why?" Daisy didn't seem to sense she was being nosy.

"Medical issues," he explained without elaborating.

"Oh." She pursed her lips about the same time her husband gave her a gentle nudge.

But apparently Daisy wasn't ready to drop the subject entirely. "Have you spoken to the elders?"

"Not yet." Actually, he hadn't really planned to, until he

came to a decision.

"They can give you wise advice," she said.

"Mmhmm." He lifted a spoonful of soup to his mouth, hoping she'd drop the subject. It seemed like people around them were beginning to eavesdrop.

Sierra shot Daisy a grateful look. Austin seemed ready to make a decision that would break her heart, and she appreciated any help in slowing him down.

Maybe she'd just been distracted, but his sermon today seemed weaker than his others had been. It had been missing the spark, the fire.

They fell silent, and Sierra began eating her lunch.

She desperately hoped Austin wouldn't leave.

During these horrible, tragic months, he had brought joy into her days. Each morning when she woke up, she had something to look forward to that day – even if it was as simple as seeing his warm eyes and matching his smile.

His gentle kisses, too few and far between, left her breathless.

The thought of losing him was like death to her.

What would she have to look forward to in this crisis-filled world?

Not much, that was for sure.

She had been hoping to marry him. Now, she could only hope he would stay here.

He hadn't asked her to consider joining him in Bolivia. He'd made no proposals about their future at all. She didn't have any status to influence his decision. He obviously cared for her, but apparently she was not relevant to this decision about his future.

Perhaps she'd misread his feelings toward her. Maybe she'd read much more into his kind words and affection than he'd intended.

They would need to have a serious conversation.

The sooner, the better.

DURING THE SUNDAY morning church service, Wu Ying's military-issued satellite telephone rang. He tried to mute it, but did not know how to silence it. Flustered, he rose and hurried out of the sanctuary.

"This is Mao Wu Ying," he answered quietly.

Lieutenant Colonel Isaac Meir, his contact with the Military Intelligence Directorate, spoke in rapid English. "We want to move you to temporary quarters here on the base. Please pack a bag. A car will arrive in ten minutes."

"But I am not at home," he protested. "It will take me fifteen minutes to get to my apartment."

"Fine. Hurry," Meir ordered. "Bring whatever you'll need for the next week."

With that, Meir terminated the call.

Wu Ying contemplated returning to the sanctuary to tell Christian and Wei Min that he would be gone for a while, but quickly ruled out the idea. They already knew he was assisting the security agencies, and they knew war was imminent. Besides, he did not wish to disrupt the service twice.

By the time he arrived home, a car was already waiting at his curb. He informed the driver he would need ten minutes to pack, and then he hurried into his apartment.

A heavy feeling settled over him as he stepped inside. War was chaotic and destructive. This very building might be bombed before he returned.

What did he really need to take with him for a week?

And what would he not want to lose, if this apartment was destroyed?

Quickly, he packed necessary clothing and basic toiletries, small electronics and chargers, then added his Bible, family photos and the remaining valuables he'd brought out of China – his wife's jewelry and some gold and silver coins. There wasn't much. His possessions were few these days.

As he exited and locked his door, he realized he was carrying the same amount of luggage with which he'd left his Beijing apartment: a carry-on suitcase and a messenger-style briefcase. He'd left his backpack behind. Hopefully he would not need it.

The driver opened the trunk, and Wu Ying placed his bags into it, then settled into the back seat and secured his seat belt. His driver wasted no time on the route to the military installation.

As they rushed past the gleaming high rises of Tel Aviv's city center, it occurred to him that he was going to be staying at a location that was a high-priority target for the enemy. Wei Min and Christian would likely be safer in their unfortified apartment building.

Wu Ying hoped he would be staying in a bunker. Also, he hoped that Israel's famed defenses, including the Iron Dome, David's Sling and Iron Beam systems, held up to their stellar reputations. If they failed, he would likely be maimed or killed.

He had read the chapters from Ezekiel that Christian had suggested last night. And while it was true that God would smite Israel's enemies, it did not say that the fighting would not be fierce.

Many lives could be lost.

Including his own.

16

After waiting another ten minutes on the Damascus airport's tarmac, Ivan's entourage finally rolled out. His vehicle was the third behind President Abramov's, and there were at least three behind him. They navigated the Syrian streets with a full contingent of police vehicles, eventually arriving at Syria's army and air force headquarters, not far from the presidential palace on Mount Mezzeh.

Syrian soldiers ushered the Russian SUVs into the headquarters. President Abramov and his staff joined waiting dignitaries from the north and eastern allies, while Ivan and the other generals entered elevators and began their descent into the bowels of the earth.

When the doors slid open, Ivan caught a whiff of slightly stale air, but as he stepped out into a gleaming hallway moments later, he noticed large ventilation fans moving fresher air into the bunker.

In the corridor, everything was white – the tile floor, the doors, the walls and even the drop ceiling. Modern LED lights in brightest white illuminated the long hall, giving the vague impression of an ethereal afterlife experience in which a person might continue down the corridor to eternity.

Fortunately, Ivan did not have that far to go. The Syrian soldiers led the way to the third set of double doors, and pushed them open. Ivan and his colleagues stepped inside.

The war room looked surprisingly familiar. It was designed and set up in a similar fashion to the one in Moscow, and Ivan suspected that was because Russian funds and expertise had been used to design and equip this facility.

Russia had long been invested in Syria, for its own reasons, and also to pose resistance to American interests there.

A sheet of standard copy paper taped at each workstation bore the name of the general to whom it was assigned. Ivan located the desk with the paper bearing his name, then he eased into the chair and booted up the computer.

He was not surprised to find the software he needed loaded and ready to go. The military intelligence technicians who had been deployed in the previous weeks had been tasked with such mundane but critical assignments.

Fatigue drifted over him as he logged into his email. He'd been up very early to catch his flight this morning, and the tension at the tarmac had worn on his nerves and energy.

Major General Nikita Pavlov settled heavily into the workstation to Ivan's right, causing his black leather chair to squeak in protest.

The old general turned to him. "Well. Here we are, once again."

"Indeed." Ivan felt a strong sense of déjà vu as the military bunker filled with war generals and their top staff. Little time had passed since Russia's previous military venture. "Hopefully this time, we will obtain a glorious victory."

"I hope so, Ivan Alexandrovich." Pavlov's watery eyes focused on him. "I expect to announce my retirement at the end of this war."

Ivan was not expecting such an announcement. He looked at his senior friend. "Then congratulations are in order. You have served Russia very well for many decades."

"I may be sorry to go," Pavlov hedged. He turned to his computer and muttered under his breath. "However, I am getting too old for this. Wars are for young men, not old ones."

Ivan could not disagree. Even he, only in his late forties but having already suffered a heart attack, might soon be getting too old for the act and art of war.

However, he hoped and expected that this war would be his last. If Russia succeeded in her goals, she would likely bask in peace for some time into the future.

If she failed... well, he would not consider that. His full focus needed to be on the successful launch, prosecution and completion of this war.

Everything in his world depended on it.

As they were finishing lunch, Austin turned to Sierra. "Can we go for a walk?"

She nodded, then sighed and picked up her soup bowl.

After taking their dishes to the kitchen, they headed outside. He offered his arm, and she silently slid her hand into the crook of his elbow. He rested his other hand on hers.

"Let's go to the overlook," he suggested.

"Okay."

He did his best to make small talk as they walked to his place, then detoured around his garden and entered the trail in the forest. He prayed silently for wisdom – both about what to do, and what to say.

Soon, they emerged on the broad rock outcropping that looked out across the Inside Passage. The waters appeared dark and stormy, like the clouds overhead. They actually matched his feelings pretty well at the moment.

He led her to a flat rock, where they both took a seat.

Sierra sighed. "It's so beautiful here."

She turned sad hazel eyes on him.

He reached for her hand. "It is."

She sighed again. "We should talk."

"I know." He shifted so he could face her directly. "This is hard."

Sierra pulled her hand away. "Are you going to break up with me?"

"I wasn't... going to." He studied her face, but it was guarded. "You don't want to break up, do you?"

"No." She frowned. "Of course not."

Relief and oxygen flooded his lungs. "Okay, good."

She eyed him silently.

He swallowed, then met her gaze. "Here's the thing. I'm really torn. I feel like I should try to go help my family, but I feel like I should stay here and pastor the church. It was Pastor Parker's final request."

She nodded, but didn't speak.

"So I'm praying about what to do." He lowered his gaze, then lifted it to hers. "Sierra, I – I want us to be together."

"Then stay," she implored. "Your dad and cousins can take care of each other. You've just accepted a call to the ministry. God wants you here."

A weak smile overtook his mouth. Austin wasn't convinced Sierra knew God's plan for his life. But he was glad she really wanted him to stay around.

"That may be," he allowed. "But if God tells me to go... would you consider coming with me?"

Her eyes widened. "To Bolivia?"

He nodded.

"What about my grandma?" She twisted her hands together. "How long would we be gone? How would I get home again?"

"I don't have those answers yet. Maybe I'm being selfish," he admitted. "Maybe it's a bad idea."

She shook her head. "No, it's not a bad idea. It's just... a little overwhelming, that's all."

SIERRA FELL SILENT. She couldn't have been more surprised if Austin had asked her to marry him. In fact... was he going to ask that?

She eyed him. He wasn't the type to invite a woman to move to another continent if he didn't intend to marry her.

Her heart pounded as she considered the possibility.

Austin turned and looked toward the water. "I'm sorry. I shouldn't have brought it up. Leaving your home and family would be too much."

It would be, unless they were getting married.

Sierra had never been to South America, but she could happily imagine hot showers and clothes dryers and tacos. Or whatever they ate in Bolivia. Apparently, the population there wasn't starving.

"It's not such a terrible idea," she said.

Or maybe it was.

While the two of them leaving would reduce the number of mouths to feed on Patmosa Island, it would also remove the only pastor and the only health care worker.

Sierra hadn't finished her nursing degree, but she'd been close... and she was the only person here with medical training beyond that of the volunteer firefighters.

It would be selfish of her to leave.

And it would be selfish to ask Austin to stay.

Her gaze dropped to her hands in her lap. They were nimble, strong hands. Over the past few months, they'd become adept at closing wounds and bandaging cuts.

They were hands of mercy, and the islanders needed them.

She swallowed, then looked at the man she'd come to love.

"I can't go, Austin." Tears rushed to her eyes, and her chin trembled. "I'm needed here."

His gaze met hers, and understanding dawned across his face. He swallowed, then nodded slowly.

"Of course. You're right."

His words unleashed the flood pressing against her eyes. She closed them tight, but a few tears escaped.

Austin pulled her to his shoulder and wrapped his arms around her. She leaned into him as sadness saturated her heart.

AT THE OUTSKIRTS of Tel Aviv, Wu Ying's car entered the military installation and proceeded through the first level of vehicle security. Stopping at the gate, the driver showed his ID and Wu Ying's, as soldiers with mirrors examined the underside of the vehicle and led a bomb-sniffing dog around it. While this was an official Aman car, it was always possible that a terrorist or traitor might have attempted to attach an explosive device to it while it was parked in the city.

After entering the first gate, the driver proceeded to the far end of the parking lot and stopped at a second security station. Again, he presented their IDs, and this time, soldiers opened the trunk and examined Wu Ying's luggage.

Minutes later, they were granted entry to an underground parking garage. The driver proceeded to the first level and parked near a set of brightly-illuminated elevators.

Wu Ying retrieved his bags and followed the officer to the elevators, which the man accessed with his military ID card. They descended two more floors. The doors opened to reveal a white-tiled hall with beige walls.

The driver led him to a door marked "-243," which he unlocked with a key card.

"This is where you will be staying." He handed the key card to Wu Ying. "Meals are served in the cafeteria at the end of this hall. If you need anything, please dial zero from the room phone. Thank you for your cooperation."

With that, he turned and strode toward the elevators.

Wu Ying entered the unlocked door and found a simple bedroom with a restroom at the far end. It reminded him of a cheap hotel, but it appeared clean and modern. He set his luggage on the bed and turned on the television.

Unless he was summoned by his handlers, he would not be getting updates from anywhere besides TV and the internet.

And since the country would be at war, information was likely to be highly censored and filled with propaganda.

He sighed as he sat on the end of the bed and flipped through the channels.

At this moment, he could not know whether he had been brought here because his assistance would be sought, or because he was deemed a threat in need of restraint. He did not expect his key card to activate the elevators or any doors other than this room and the cafeteria.

Essentially, he was a prisoner here, but he chose not to be

offended by that. He was new to Israel, and his loyalties were not yet fully proven.

17

The next morning, a beeping alarm rousted Ivan from a restless night's sleep. His accommodations in the bunker were adequate but far from luxurious. His small suite featured one bed, a nightstand, a small table with two chairs and a bowl of fruit, a refrigerator and microwave oven, and a cramped washroom across from a narrow, open closet.

He glanced at the clock. Two a.m. local time, which was two hours behind Tobolsk. He'd gotten nearly seven hours of sleep. And he'd needed every minute of it, because today would be long and stressful.

The war was set to launch two hours from now.

In less than thirty minutes, he was showered, dressed and ready for work. He grabbed an apple from the bowl of fresh fruit on the table, and ate it as he walked down the hall to the elevator. His suite was located one floor above the war rooms.

Entering the elevator, he pushed the button for the lower floor, and considered how fantastic it was that all of the allies had been persuaded, and all of the war preparations had come together in so little time.

Each of the regional allies had its own military war room on the same floor as Russia's, and language translators had been gathered to ensure swift and accurate communication between them.

Russia was running this show, but all of the allies had their own part to play in it.

As he stepped out of the elevator, the fragrance of food hit him, but it was not particularly enticing. It smelled as if the catering staff had brought in a mix of Russian and Middle Eastern breakfast entrees, sparking a clashing aroma of spicy, sour, sweet and savory.

He entered the double doors for the Russian war room, and noted the food service workers setting up breakfast tables at the back of the room. White linen draped four tables set up buffet style, with tea and other beverages on the first table.

Ivan's stomach grumbled, and he detoured to collect a cup of black tea, a boiled egg, and a bowl of warm, sweet kasha. These he carried on a small tray to his desk, where he ate as he logged into his computer and checked his email.

As he made his first phone calls, his colleagues began filling the room. They kept their voices low as they conversed or issued orders to their subordinates.

At three a.m., one hour before the planned launch of hostilities, President Abramov entered from a side door at the front of the room.

Ivan ended his call with Colonel Lev Balakin, and focused his attention on the leader of the Russian Federation.

President Abramov made his way to a small lectern at the front of the room. Behind and above him, three large screens hung on the wall. The first screen featured satellite imagery of the region, with Israel's borders marked in red. The middle screen and the one on the right were not yet illuminated.

"Gentlemen, we are about to embark on what I expect will

be Russia's greatest conquest in a thousand years." The president paused and eyed his military leaders. "Our invasion is set to begin in one hour, and it is my understanding that everything is ready for a successful launch. If anything is amiss, please announce it at this time."

He stopped and waited. No one spoke.

President Abramov squared his shoulders. "Excellent. Then I will leave you to your final preparations. May you all find glory in this venture, and may you bring much glory to Russia!"

Mild applause accompanied his departure from the lectern, and Ivan turned to his computer screen.

From his perspective, everything was in order. The men were in place, the materiel was ready, the bombs were loaded and the missiles were targeted. There was nothing left to do but wait and watch the clock tick down the minutes to launch.

After the longest hour Ivan could remember, the clock finally indicated 4 a.m.

Energy surged through his body and mind. He drew a sharp breath.

It was time for war!

At the front of the room, President Abramov looked at his generals and gave a single nod.

"Commence the battle."

Ivan communicated the directive to his Ground Forces staff at the same time as his colleagues gave the order to their various divisions and departments.

The mood in the bunker was electric.

Ivan's body practically buzzed with excitement.

There was a deep thrill in launching a military endeavor, and it was one he might never tire of. He glanced over at General Pavlov and saw the tension in the old man's neck and jaw. No wonder the man had not yet retired. A successful battle carried a high like cocaine – and was equally addicting.

At the front of the room, the center screen and the one on the right came to life. The one in the middle depicted troop and equipment placements on Israel's border with Syria, and the one on the right showed the allies' battle formations on Israel's border with Egypt.

Soon, those troops would push forward across the borders.

But first, Russia and her friends were launching airstrikes to soften the enemy's lines.

Israel's military was first-class, and her Iron Dome was a brilliant piece of defense. Not to mention her David's Sling and Iron Beam systems. This war would not be easy, but it would be worth it.

WHEN AUSTIN ARRIVED at the communications shack on Monday morning, he found a large crowd already assembled. His shoulders tensed. This couldn't be good. Maybe Canada was planning on dropping off hundreds of American citizens at the Hideaway dock today.

"What's going on?"

"Another war!" Daisy exclaimed. "Russia and her allies are invading Israel, like in your sermon yesterday."

Alfred had tuned his shortwave radio to pick up an international broadcast in English. A female reporter with a thick British accent described the conflict in the Middle East.

"For many weeks, Russia, Iran, Egypt and their allied countries have been building up military equipment and troops in the Middle East and running cooperative war drills. This morning, the forces attacked Israel on two fronts. The tiny country has mounted a strong defense, but they seem likely to be overrun."

Austin rubbed his jaw. He glanced toward the doorway in time to see Sierra enter. She beelined to him with a huge question on her face.

"The first Gog and Magog war has begun," he whispered, wrapping an arm around her shoulders.

The British reporter continued. "Russia and her allies are pounding Israel's lines of defense with volley after volley of rockets and missiles. Israeli forces are returning fire, but they appear to be taking heavy losses. Early reports from official sources in the nation present a more optimistic picture than we are seeing from satellite feeds and independent reports in Israel."

The woman paused for a moment, then said, "We are also receiving conflicting reports on the success or inadequacy of Israel's vaunted Iron Dome, Iron Beam and other defensive systems. It's too soon to make a definitive call, but it appears those defenses are being sorely stressed at this time."

She inhaled a noisy breath and rushed on. "Our analysts say that an Israeli victory is possible but unlikely. They expect she will run out of conventional weapons, at this rate, in less than a week. Of course, it has long been believed that Israel has nuclear weapons, but it is unclear whether her leaders would be willing to use them right on their own borders – or inside them, if it comes to that."

Austin tensed. Sierra leaned into him.

He had always expected to live to see the end times, but it was still astonishing to listen via radio as the long-anticipated Gog and Magog war came to pass.

As the journalist continued her report, his gaze drifted to the clocks on the wall. It was seven o'clock. Time for his cousins to check in. He hated to interrupt the news broadcast, but he needed to know if his family was coming to the island today.

He released his grip on Sierra's shoulders and leaned toward Alfred.

"It's time for my family to check in," he said quietly. "Can you dial that up while still leaving the radio on for everybody else?"

Alfred shook his head. "Nope. Too noisy in here with the shortwave running through the speakers. You'll be shouting over it."

The old radio operator glanced at the gathered group.

"Sorry. Need turn off the news for a few minutes."

This was met with numerous objections, but he waved them off. "Austin had an appointment. The rest of you can come back in ten minutes. Not much is gonna change with a war in that time."

Austin hoped Alfred was right about that.

If this truly was the first Gog and Magog war, ten minutes might make all the difference in the world.

As the communications building emptied out, Sierra remained behind with Austin to hear what his family would say. Surely they would check in this morning and let him know whether or not they were coming. She took one of the empty chairs and settled in to wait. It shouldn't be long.

Alfred put on his headphones, fiddled with his radio, said a few words, and then turned suddenly to Austin.

"I've got their ham operator." He removed the headphone cord from the jack and sent the sound through the speakers. "You're on."

Sierra straightened in her chair. Her upper body tensed.

She didn't know what to hope for – if Austin's family had decided to go to Bolivia, he would likely leave. On the other hand, if they came here, that opened a huge can of worms. She didn't know how the community would safely accommodate a paranoid schizophrenic.

"This is Austin," he said. "Are my cousins there with you?"

"No, they aren't." The man sounded put out. "They had an appointment to be here ten minutes ago, but they haven't shown up yet."

Sierra studied Austin's expression.

He looked baffled. "I'm sorry. I'm not sure what to say. That's not like them."

"People are unpredictable these days," the gruff operator said. "I suppose you heard about the new war this morning?"

"We did," Austin answered. "But about my cousins... do you know where they're staying? Can you check up on them?"

"No and no. If they show up here again, I'll be in touch. Lately, lots of folks just seem to disappear."

"That's not like them," Austin insisted. "They made a long trip across the continent to get here. I'm sure something happened, or they would have been at your place this morning."

"If you say so." Skepticism flooded his voice.

Austin met Sierra's gaze. After a moment, he turned back to the microphone. "I'll look forward to hearing from them soon. Thank you for your time."

"Sure." The man signed off, and the room fell silent.

Austin rose from his chair. Wordlessly, he walked to the small eastern window and gazed out, then ran both hands through his black hair.

Sierra's lungs constricted. Something about all this wasn't right.

Why hadn't his family made their scheduled appointment

with the radio operator? Had they been hurt? Injured or killed?

Civilization was still somewhat stable here on Patmosa Island, but she'd heard of all kinds of atrocious crimes happening on the North American continent. As law enforcement collapsed, criminals targeted the rest of society. Even people who had not been violent prior to the war and tsunami became outright predators when they realized that their crimes would go unpunished. In this world, anyway.

Austin turned from the window and looked at the old radio operator.

"Thanks, Alfred. I appreciate it."

Then he glanced at Sierra. "I'm headed out. You want to come, or you want to stay and listen to the war news?"

She'd heard enough of war.

"I'll come with you."

As they stepped outside, they were met with questioning looks on their friends' faces.

"That was awful quick," Daisy said. "Is your family on their way?"

"Not sure," Austin answered. "They missed their appointment with the ham operator."

"Oh." She frowned slightly, then relaxed. "I imagine they'll either show up on the transport, or they'll be in touch soon."

"I expect so," he agreed. "Meanwhile, you all can go back to listening to the war news on the radio."

The mayor glanced toward the radio building.

"Now hold on," he said. "We've got our own major problem. Whether or not Austin's relatives are coming, the Canadian government is set to push a bunch of folks on us today. And we still haven't resolved what we're going to do about that."

NEAR TEL AVIV, a blaring alarm had rousted Wu Ying from his slumber at 4 a.m. He had no doubt what this meant.

The country was under attack.

He reached for the television's remote control and turned on the propaganda device. Generally, he could sort through official lies to get to some underlying truth in the newscasts.

On the screen, brilliant streaks of light illuminated a dark sky, accompanied by muted sounds of war's explosions.

Israel was being clobbered by missiles and drones, and her defense shields were up. He watched as the Iron Dome sent up one volley of interceptor missiles after another. It appeared the David's Sling System was also in play, launching Stunner missiles at low altitude. He noted the Iron Beam lasers were active, as well.

A female reporter explained the situation in rapid Hebrew, which was no help to Wu Ying, so he reduced the volume.

He recognized the Tel Aviv skyline. Then, as the video feed was switched, he saw the golden Dome of the Rock in Jerusalem.

For some reason, seeing the ancient city under missile attack made his heart ache and his spirit rage.

He thought he should care more for Tel Aviv, his current home and that of his friends. But no, his greater concern was for the welfare of Jerusalem.

Suddenly, he remembered a Psalm he had recently read.

Reaching for his Bible, he flipped through the chapters until he found it – Psalm 122. He knelt on the floor beside his bed and read verses six through nine aloud, as a prayer.

"Pray for the peace of Jerusalem:
'May they prosper who love you.
Peace be within your walls,

Prosperity within your palaces.'
For the sake of my brethren and companions,
I will now say, 'Peace *be* within you.'
Because of the house of the LORD our God
I will seek your good."

Wu Ying turned off the television and prayed earnestly for Jerusalem and Israel. He had no doubt God heard his prayers and that of millions of others around the world.

Although the situation appeared grim while ravenous enemies surrounded and attacked the tiny nation, he held onto the hope provided by the prophet Ezekiel over 2,500 years ago. In this war, the Lord would come to the aid of the Jews and rescue their country.

If God did not intervene, Wu Ying could not see how Israel could prevail. From his military perspective, they were surrounded, outnumbered and doomed.

18

As the day progressed, Ivan monitored the progress of the war on his computer and the large display screens in the bunker.

Squadrons of fighter jets engaged in air battles above the two front lines. In the sky, Israel held her own. Equipped with the newest technology and flown by experienced pilots, the Jews were able to fend off attacks in the air.

The ground was a different matter, and this was Ivan's place. As leader of Ground Forces, he viewed the attacks and advances as something of a game of chess – he would sacrifice some of his pawns to seize an Israeli rook or bishop.

As he saw it, the weakness of Israel's Iron Dome and other defensive systems was their saturation point, which was a number not known to foreigners. But an Iron Dome battery could only deal with a certain number of incoming threats at a time before it became overwhelmed, and the excess threats would get through and reach their targets.

Each Iron Dome battery defended a small region of the country, and each battery could only deal with a certain number of threats before reaching its saturation point.

Ivan's plan was to exceed those unknown saturation points with a profuse barrage of weaponry, including missiles and drones.

Russia and her allies spent the first nine hours of the war bombarding Israel's defenses with swarms of drones and cheap rockets. For each one they sent over the border, an Iron Dome, Iron Beam or other defense system automatically calculated trajectories and targets, then instantaneously determined whether or not to target that incoming threat.

That worked great for fending off attacks from homemade rockets inbound to Tel Aviv from the Arabs in the Gaza Strip – but it did not work so well today, with modern drones that zigged and zagged and did not reveal their target via their trajectory.

Ivan took a sip of tea that had cooled in its cup. His plan entailed overwhelming the enemy's defenses through saturation – to inundate them with more drones, missiles and rockets than they could adequately defend against.

So far, that appeared to be working.

Russia and her allies were making slow but steady progress softening both front lines. Within hours, he expected to be able to send tanks and troops over the Syrian border. Judging by the progress he watched on the screens at the front of the bunker, he expected Egypt to be leading the charge across Israel's southern border shortly thereafter.

Ivan was pleased.

The war was not going perfectly, but it was going very well.

In fact, as the day wore on, he grew steadily more encouraged.

His plan had been brilliant.

It was working, and he would be lauded for this.

By mid-afternoon, his colleagues appeared noticeably less stressed. Even old Pavlov held his head high and his shoulders back as he wore an expression that could only be described as pride in accomplishment.

Ivan wondered if the old war dog would actually retire after this war. He should, of course. Pavlov was still mentally sharp, but he was getting too old for this work. And several younger men quietly chafed to be seated in his chair.

As he worked, Ivan ate lightly. He had skipped lunch, but grazed on fruit and a pastry or two. Now, as the afternoon ground on, he looked forward to a full meal.

He'd earned it.

Maybe he would even celebrate the day's successes with a sip of vodka.

OUTSIDE THE RADIO BUILDING, Austin looked at Mayor Williams. The world was at war with Israel, his own family might be missing or victimized, and the mayor was worried about some U.S. citizens who may or may not show up on the island today.

"We don't even know if anyone's coming," he pointed out.

"Actually, we do." The mayor hooked his thumbs in his suspenders, which were becoming a popular accessory since everyone was losing weight. "Early this morning, I asked Alfred to get in touch with the Canadian officials, and they reported that nineteen people had signed up for today's transport to Patmosa."

The mayor's eyes bugged slightly. "Nineteen people! Where are we going to put them up? What are we going to feed them? They'll need Alaska gear – waterproof coats and pants, boots, winter coats and so on. And this is only the first transport. Who knows how many more there will be?"

Austin wasn't thrilled about having a lot of new folks

arrive, either, but his own family was likely to be among them. Perhaps that was why they missed the radio appointment this morning – maybe they decided there wasn't time to go to their ham operator's studio and still make it to the boarding location in time for departure.

He breathed a sigh. Yeah, that was probably it.

As for the fifteen other people on the transport – he was glad to hear it was only fifteen, actually. That was a lot, but it could have been more. Fifty, or even a hundred!

What would the Lord have them do about these new folks?

The Bible had a lot to say about hospitality. He tried to recall some of it.

Jake Williams rubbed the back of his neck. "I say we have one more quick meeting right away. See if we can come up with a plan."

The group voiced its general approval.

Laszlo Koval gave a nod. "We can meet in the fellowship hall. Please spread the word, so everybody knows."

Austin glanced at Sierra.

She slid her hand into his. "Can we talk?"

"Of course." He gave her hand a squeeze. "Let's go to the greenhouse."

They left the crowd and started toward the big structure.

Inside, the fickle sun had warmed the greenhouse about fifteen degrees higher than the outside temperature.

Sierra turned those big eyes on him. "What are you going to do, Austin? If your family doesn't get in touch?"

"I'm sure they will. They'll probably show up on the transport today."

"What if they don't?" She ran her fingers through the ends of her long brown hair.

"Then I'll expect them to radio in and let me know what's going on."

SIERRA FELT like Austin wasn't getting her point. "But what if they don't do that, either? I mean... well, it's possible something happened to them."

"What are you suggesting?"

"Crime. Accident. I don't know." She resisted the urge to scratch her head.

Austin sat down on a short bench. "I hope that didn't happen."

"If you don't hear anything, what will you do?"

"What can I do?" He gave her a confused look. "I'll try to make radio contact. I'll hope they check in. I'll pray for their safety."

She drew in a deep breath. "Okay. Good."

"Was there something else you think I should do?" He studied her with those serious dark eyes.

"No. I was just wondering if you'd try to go find them."

He shook his head.

"I don't think so. It'd be very difficult getting to Prince Rupert. And if the worst has happened... there'd be nothing I could do about it." Austin eyed her. "Right?"

"Right." Tension eased from her shoulders. Austin wasn't going anywhere. At least, not right away.

He pulled a weed from a tomato pot. "I'll try to reach my dad. Maybe he's heard something from them. It's possible they've caught a flight to Bolivia."

"Already?" It struck her as unlikely, given the difficulties in Canada since the tsunami.

"Maybe they found flights. They might be driving to a larger city to catch a plane." He sighed, then looked at her. "I have no idea, Sierra."

"I hope they're okay," she offered.

"Yeah. Let's pray for them." He held out both hands to her, and she gripped them as he began his prayer.

She had a hard time focusing.

So many things were happening all at once. The confusion about his cousins, the war in the Middle East, the anticipated influx of new residents on the island... nineteen homeless would be a big enough challenge. What were her neighbors going to do if hundreds of new people arrived in the coming weeks?

AROUND 3 P.M., a sharp rap resounded on Wu Ying's door. He turned off the television and hurried to see who was there.

Two Aman intelligence officers waited in the corridor. Both wore perfectly neat uniforms and bland expressions, but he could see the tension in their eyes.

"You have been summoned," one said. "Please come with us."

Wu Ying did not bother asking questions. He could not expect these men to provide any answers. Soon enough, he would know what this was about.

The officers led him to the elevator, where they descended one floor, then emerged into a hall that smelled faintly of floor cleaner. They took him to the end of the hall, turned the corner, and entered a small room where four men sat around a large table.

Wu Ying recognized one man, his handler, Lieutenant Colonel Isaac Meir. He did not know the other men, and no one bothered to introduce him. From their uniform insignias, he noted they were all of high rank in the intelligence corps.

"Please have a seat," Meir urged, motioning to the end of the table.

Wu Ying sat, his back rigid and feet flat on the floor.

"Have you been following today's events?" Meir asked.

"Yes. On the television."

"Fine. We've brought you here to see if you can offer any more insight on the Russian major general, Ivan Orlov. All evidence indicates he designed this allied attack, and of course, as leader of Ground Forces, he is in charge of much of it."

Wu Ying nodded. "I hope I can be of some help."

"You can." Meir glanced at his colleagues before looking at Wu Ying. "If you can think of any weaknesses – personal or professional – that might help."

Wu Ying inhaled slowly as he considered this. "I do not know him well personally, but in my professional dealings with him, I have sensed... some pride. I believe he exercises care in reigning it in or disguising it, but nevertheless, it is there."

One of the men Wu Ying did not know eyed him. "That is not surprising in a man with his accomplishments."

Of course it wasn't. But it was a chink in the man's armor, nevertheless. Wu Ying chose not to respond to the comment. A wise person would know that any personal flaws could be exploited, given the right angle of attack. Perhaps this officer was not particularly wise.

"That could prove helpful." Meir leaned back in his chair and studied Wu Ying. "Now, given what you know of Major General Orlov, how would you expect him to proceed, following an initial attack that appears to be going in his favor? Will he advance with strategic caution, moving to preserve his forces and equipment for a potentially long war? Will he rush forward, throwing caution to the wind? Will he advance as far as possible as quickly as he can?"

Wu Ying only needed a moment to consider his answer.

"From my interaction with him, I would expect him to press his attack with great speed," he said. "I think he will push ahead quickly, attempting to break across Israel's border today, and pushing as far as he can all night and tomorrow. His troops will get little rest. I expect he will send waves of troops – as many as he possibly can – against Israel's defenses to overwhelm your army."

"I see." Meir leaned forward. "How many do you think he might send in the first day?"

To answer that, Wu Ying needed more information. "How many do you estimate that he and his allies have on the ground in the region?"

The Israeli officer swallowed before he responded.

"A million."

"There is your answer," Wu Ying said. "He will send them all, or as many as he can push through Israel's mountains."

19

A s evening approached, Ivan found himself thrilled with the progress of the war. He had planned to take an early dinner, but things were going so well on the Syrian front that his troops were ready to invade across the border.

He couldn't miss a moment of this.

The bunker quieted as the screens on the front wall depicted aerial views of Russian tanks charging Israel's front line.

The Jews blasted them with their best artillery, killing many of the tanks.

But others clawed their way forward, reaching the Jewish positions. More followed in their tracks, evading the anti-tank defenses and fortifications, and charging the front.

Less than an hour later, similar advances could be seen on the southern front, as Egypt led the allies' charge against Israel's border there.

Ivan's stomach rumbled a demand for dinner, but he ignored it. He could eat any time.

What he was witnessing – what he was leading – was historic!

The last time the Jews had been overrun and displaced from their own land was in 70 A.D.

It had been nearly two thousand years since anyone else had done what he was doing here, today!

As he watched, Russian tanks pushed forward in a massive rush on Israel's border.

Slowly, slowly, then suddenly, the Israelis began to fall back.

They were ceding territory to the Russian invaders!

A roar filled the bunker, and Ivan's voice joined in.

This was a day of triumph!

A day that would go down in history forever.

Ivan would be recognized for his success. He had formulated this joint plan of allied action, and it was working better than he could have imagined.

In a few weeks – perhaps even days – he would be walking in triumph in the streets of Jerusalem.

His chest swelled, irritating the scar tissue from his heart surgery.

Marina would be so proud.

Nina would be delightfully happy when he arrived home, a true national hero. Even Anton, the volatile teenager, would be the star of his school. The future would be wide open for his children, and for their children after them.

He took a sip of water.

In the space of only a few months, Russia had climbed from the depths of despair to the pinnacle of success.

And he, Ivan, had led the way.

But that was not all.

Everyone who mattered knew it.

As if to validate that thought, Pavlov approached, his old

blue eyes twinkling. He gave Ivan a firm pat on the back and a solid nod of approval.

Moments later, other colleagues gathered around.

It was a moment that called for a toast.

However, there was still much work to be done, and President Abramov would surely not approve of such a celebration that did not center around himself. Not that it mattered. The president could bask in the glory of this success as well. He had championed Ivan's plan, after all.

There was plenty of glory to go around, for all of them.

APPROACHING the doors of the fellowship hall, Austin joined the group gathering for Mayor Williams' last-minute meeting prior to the arrival of the newcomers. Sierra entered with him, and they found seats near the middle of the room. Moments later, her grandmother arrived and settled in beside them.

"I don't know why we have so many meetings," Mrs. Forester groused. "But I hate to miss any. Something important might go down."

"Exactly." Austin smiled at her. "If nothing else, they're good entertainment, right?"

She chuckled. "Aside from books and board games, they're practically the only entertainment we have these days!"

Sierra leaned forward and caught her grandma's eye. "I'm glad you made it. You often have the best input."

"Flattery will get you nowhere, young lady," she teased.

"Bummer. I was hoping for bear steaks for lunch tomorrow."

"You got it." Mrs. Forester winked at her granddaughter, then glanced at Austin. "You want to join us for that?"

"I'd love to." He paused. "Depending on what's happening with my family."

At the front of the room, the mayor called for attention. "Let's get started, if we may."

Austin drew in a deep breath. He wasn't sure if anything could be resolved here, but he hoped any decisions or outcomes would honor the Lord.

The Patmosa Island community had only made it this far due to the Lord's blessing and the strong Christian leadership of Fellowship Farm's elders. The rest of Alaska, lacking the godly direction and divine blessing, had apparently suffered nearly as badly as the other states, with rampant starvation, disease and death.

If his Patmosa neighbors turned aside from honoring God, surely they'd end up in the same predicament.

Before coming to this meeting, he'd looked up several scriptures that related to hosting strangers or showing hospitality, and the Bible was clear: such kindness was expected from those who claimed to follow Christ.

This went against Austin's nature, and against his background as a hermit, when he'd cherished his privacy and time alone with God. Still, scripture was plain – Christians were to be kind, generous and hospitable people.

As the room quieted, Mayor Williams smiled at the assembled group.

"Thank you all for coming. I know it's short notice, but we have nineteen people arriving today and we still have not determined how to handle that as a community."

A murmur rippled through the room at this announcement. While everyone knew that there was a transport scheduled, this was probably the first time they'd heard the official refugee number for the initial group of arrivals.

Nineteen might not sound like a lot – but for a tiny

community like this, it would be a big stretch. And who knew? Waves of new arrivals might soon follow this trickle, as word got out that Patmosa Island was the only remaining viable community in Alaska.

AS THE MEETING PROGRESSED, Sierra listened to her neighbors' many concerns, but there was no way to solve those problems. These people, who might be criminals or predators or sick or contagious, were coming.

Today.

At a pause in the conversation, she raised her hand. When the mayor looked at her, she stood to ask a question.

"Should we quarantine them? They might have lice or bedbugs or communicable diseases. For many years, newcomers to a region went through a medical exam or quarantine so they didn't infect the local residents with their medical issues."

"Good point," a local farmer agreed. "We do that with new animals. You don't just put them in with your established herd, until you've quarantined them and are pretty sure they're not carrying a disease."

The mayor nodded. "Yes, that's a good point. Thanks for bringing it up."

He glanced around the room. "Anybody else want to address this?"

"I will." Daisy stood up. She looked at Sierra. "A medical exam is a good idea. Could you do that? I'd volunteer to help."

"I...." Sierra wasn't sure her unfinished medical education was sufficient. "I guess we could do a basic exam. Medical questionnaire, take temperatures, listen to lungs and hearts. Basic observations."

"Don't forget the lice," Grandma interjected with a shudder.

"You can help me with that," Sierra said. "And look through their luggage for bedbugs."

"Good heavens." Grandma sighed. "I can't believe it's come to that. Bedbugs were eradicated in the United States!"

"Not anymore," Sierra pointed out. "They came back."

"Because of illegal aliens," someone shouted from the back of the room.

The mayor scowled at that remark. "Okay, I think we've addressed the medical exams. Thank you for volunteering, ladies. Sierra, do you think a quarantine is necessary?"

"It would be ideal," she answered, "but I'm not sure if it's realistic. Would they submit to an unexpected quarantine? If not, would we hold them against their will?"

"Absolutely not," Austin objected. "That's like false imprisonment."

She met his gaze. "No, it isn't. Quarantines have historically been used to control the spread of disease and protect the local populations from imported illness... or death. Anyway, it's only temporary. It's not like they're in jail forever."

"How long, Sierra?" Mayor Williams asked.

"Thirty days is ideal, but ten days will ferret out most illnesses that are incubating."

"Ten days isn't too bad," the mayor said. "To protect the entire community. Right, Austin?"

The quiet hermit rubbed his chin, then looked from Sierra to the mayor. "I suppose."

"Good." Mayor Williams nodded. "That's a plan, then. A medical exam and a ten-day quarantine. If they don't like it, they can continue on to the next town."

Grandma raised her hand. "Where are we going to keep them for this quarantine?"

The room fell silent. People looked at their friends and neighbors for answers. Finally, Laszlo Koval stood up.

"I think the elders will approve of letting them use the recreation hall. We can set up cots again, like we did for the Hideaway residents after the tsunami. We can deliver meals there from the kitchen."

"Perfect." Mayor Williams smiled. "That kills two birds with one stone – the quarantine issue, and the question of where to house the newcomers – at least for a while."

AFTER MEETING with Lieutenant Colonel Isaac Meir and his colleagues, Wu Ying was escorted back to his temporary quarters on the military base.

He sat on the end of his bed and stared at the black television screen.

Did he want to turn it on and see how badly the war was progressing for Israel?

Not really.

And yet, his curiosity compelled him.

He picked up the remote and pressed the power button.

The screen flared to life. In saturated color, battle scenes played out on the background, while a reporter appeared behind a desk in the foreground.

Wu Ying scrolled through the channels, and finally found one with English subtitles. He suspected the broadcasts approved to be shown on the military base were limited to those acceptable to the Israeli government.

His attention flickered between reading the subtitles and watching the video images. Between the two, it was easy to come to the conclusion that Israel was putting up a valiant defense.

Presumably, that meant the attackers had the upper hand in the battle.

As he watched and read, he became more and more convinced that the Jews were taking a vicious beating. Their borders were already being breached and their country was being invaded at this moment.

Because it was such a tiny country geographically, it was reasonable to expect that the invaders could be on the doorstep of Jerusalem or Tel Aviv by tomorrow morning.

He turned off the television.

The prophecy in Ezekiel indicated that the Lord would fight this battle for His people. If that was the case, Wu Ying hoped God would not delay His intervention.

Israel's front lines appeared to be on the brink of collapse.

There wasn't anything Wu Ying could do about it.

Except pray.

He sank to his knees on the tan carpet, folded his hands, closed his eyes and bowed his head.

Oh, Lord, help us. Come to the aid of Your people. Fulfill the prophecy given to Your servant Ezekiel. Please, Lord, spare us. In Jesus' holy name. Amen.

20

W hile his stomach complained about delaying dinner, Ivan monitored the status of his troops. Even now, they flooded across Israel's northeastern border like a great tsunami of warriors. Tens of thousands of soldiers poured into Israel's mountain region, with hundreds of thousands right behind them.

He saw similar success on the southern front.

By nightfall, Russia and her allies would securely hold territory fifty kilometers or more inside Israel's borders.

Tomorrow, they might reach Tel Aviv and Jerusalem.

He could barely believe the tremendous success of this venture!

A hand touched his shoulder and he turned, expecting to find a colleague, but instead looked into the steady gaze of President Abramov. The man gave him a genuine smile, then he glanced around at his military leaders.

"Gentlemen, this has been a glorious day. Let us celebrate with a festive dinner, and be sure to acknowledge Major General Orlov, who originally devised this clever and highly successful plan."

As his colleagues applauded, Ivan rose to his feet, gave a gracious nod to the president, and then accepted the honor of applause.

"Thank you." He nodded humbly. "Thank you very much."

Then, turning to the president, he extended his hand, sharing the praise with the political leader.

President Abramov lifted his hand to calm the clapping. When silence reigned, he said, "We have caterers bringing a fine dinner here to the bunker. We might have found a more elegant location, but seeing as this is the first day of the war, you may wish to remain close to your desks for contact with your subordinates."

He turned to Ivan.

"Please join me at my table." He gestured toward the front of the room, where servers were setting a small table with white linens and fresh flowers.

Ivan gave a single nod. "I would be honored."

As they walked toward the table, a strange moan filled the room. Ivan looked around for the source of the noise, which was followed by a thunderous boom.

His legs gave out from under him as everything seemed to jerk sideways.

He fell, landing hard on his left hip.

Pain shot up his spine.

Was he having a stroke?

Attempting to scramble to his feet, he braced himself with his left hand and pushed off the floor, only to fall again as shouts filled the bunker.

Computer monitors crashed to the tile floor, adding to the confusion, as the floor jerked and bucked.

"Bomb!" A colleague shouted, stumbling toward the exit.

A great jolt sent desks and tables careening to the left side of the room, dumping computers and food all over the floor.

Some people remained in their chairs as they sailed into the left wall.

Pavlov's empty chair smashed into Ivan.

Men yelped and yelled.

Moments later, desks, computers and chairs, along with the preparations for dinner, flew back in the opposite direction, smashing into men as they went.

The corner of a desk struck Ivan's back as he attempted to get out of the way.

Pavlov hollered as President Abramov's dinner table pinned him to the far wall. Ivan struggled to his feet and tried to make his way to the old man.

Thunderous booms competed with crashing noises and the wails and groans of the men.

The bunker lurched and moaned, then jolted again, and Ivan was tossed into a heap of chairs.

Cries of injured men filled the room.

One of those cries rose from his own throat.

IN THE FELLOWSHIP HALL, Austin glanced at the clock on the wall as the meeting finally wound down. The refugees should be arriving in less than two hours. He needed to be down at the Hideaway dock by then to meet his family. If they arrived.

At the front of the room, the mayor smiled at the gathered group.

"One last issue, then we'll wrap this up," he promised. "In addition to the medical team – Sierra and her grandmother and Daisy – we'll need a welcoming committee. And I think they should be armed."

Austin controlled the urge to roll his eyes. "How is that *welcoming*, exactly?"

"I'm glad you asked. These refugees should know that they will be welcome here as long as they follow the rules. Go through the medical exam, agree to quarantine, and so on. Also, they should feel safer knowing the locals are prepared to protect them from predators of either type... two-legged or four-legged."

"Hear, hear," a woman agreed from the back of the room.

Austin disagreed. "It sounds like an awfully bristly welcome, if you ask me."

"Nobody invited these people here," the mayor reminded him. "Except you. And you only invited your family members."

That wasn't exactly true. Austin's family had *informed* him they were coming. He wasn't sure he'd actually invited them. But he wasn't going to quibble over details.

"Besides," the mayor added, "there might be serious criminals among the group arriving today. If they see we're all armed and ready to defend ourselves, they might move along."

Austin frowned. "To another Southeast community. That's sending trouble on to our fellow Alaskans."

"Not my problem," Mayor Williams responded. "And not my fault. Again, we didn't ask for all these new folks to come and park on us. But they're coming, so we've got to deal with them."

He turned to the rest of the assembly. "Okay, any volunteers for the welcoming committee?"

Several men raised their hands. Austin did, too, but he planned to keep his grizzly-chewed handgun concealed. He needed to be at the dock anyway, to greet his family and to protect Sierra and the other ladies from any violent criminals.

Mrs. Forester raised her hand. "What about transportation? It's a long walk down to Hideaway, and seems even longer coming back up the mountain."

Several folks chuckled.

"Not only that," she added, "but what if these folks are bringing stuff like luggage or furniture?"

Austin blinked. That was a good point. His family had been traveling in a car, so he knew they wouldn't have furniture, but what if they brought eight suitcases? Nobody wanted to drag those uphill for a few miles. Besides, Grandpa would have a difficult time making the hike up to the farm.

He glanced at Tom Johnson. "You're going to run your taxi, right?"

"Sure. At regular prices." The man nodded. "But there's obviously no room for furniture, and luggage is going to cost extra, since it will take up passenger space and require more trips."

The mayor smiled. "Fair enough. Thank you, Tom."

He adjourned the meeting and released the restless audience.

Austin rose and stretched his back.

Beside him, Mrs. Forester stood up slowly. "That was a doggone long meeting! I think arthritis froze all my joints."

Sierra laughed. "You don't have arthritis, Grandma."

"I might." She rolled her shoulders. "I'm stiff, anyway."

Sierra rubbed Grandma's shoulders for a moment, then turned to Austin. "I need to gather a few things in a medical bag to take down to the dock. Are you walking or riding with Tom?"

Before he could answer, Grandma interjected, "You should

take your truck, Austin. That way you can drive your family and all their gear back up to the farm."

He shook his head.

"I'm not even sure they'll be there. And once I run out of gas, that's it. So it's emergencies only for that old clunker." He turned to Sierra. "I think I'll walk down. Maybe I'll ride back up. Then I'll only have to pay for a one-way trip. I'm getting tired of splitting Tom's firewood for him."

She chuckled. Tom charged for rides in his golf-cart taxi according to what he needed or wanted done. For Austin, that meant chopping wood. For Sierra, it was usually weeding his garden.

She hated weeding.

"I hear ya. I'll walk down, too. Give me a minute to get my medical gear."

"I'll see you both when you get down there," Grandma said. "I'm riding for sure. It costs me a pint of blueberry jam, but that's worth it!"

Sierra shot Austin a look. "I think Tom's going to make a killing today."

He nodded. "If he can keep his taxi running."

Tom charged his golf cart batteries using a mix of solar and wind power. He might need to stop and recharge them today. Eventually, his batteries would die, but until then, he was set. In exchange for rides up and down the island, he had people who did most of the work around his house, and provided dinners and snacks.

Of all the folks on Patmosa Island, Tom was the only one who still looked a little portly.

Sierra went upstairs to a small storage room at the back of the chapel, where she stored some of the community's medical supplies. She gathered a thermometer, gloves, rubbing alcohol, wipes, stethoscope, otoscope, tongue depressors, pen light and some other essentials, then added a clip-board, paper and pens. All the gear went into a backpack, along with her water bottle and rain coat.

She hurried outside to meet Austin, and found him waiting under a tree by the parking lot.

"Ready?" She smiled at him.

"I guess I am." He offered his arm, and she slid her hand into the crook of his elbow.

They walked out the driveway, and as they approached his little shack, his steps slowed.

"I need to get a few things," he said. "It'll just take a minute."

"No rush. Take your time."

She waited outside as he went in to gather his gear. It was a nice day, for Southeast Alaska. No rain, only a slight overcast, which the sun broke through occasionally.

She should savor this time, because big changes were on the horizon.

If Austin's family arrived, he would have less time for her. He'd be busier, hosting and caring for his grandfather and schizophrenic nephew. He would need to focus on securing local housing for them after their quarantine ended.

Still, losing some time with him would be far preferable to having him move to Bolivia, even if she did accompany him there – which she really couldn't, due to her medical responsi-bilities here on the island.

Besides, she could not imagine being away from all her lifelong friends and neighbors, not to mention McKenna and Grandma, during such a turbulent period of time in history. And she'd desperately miss flamboyant, curly-haired Daisy, too.

"Ready?" Austin stepped out of his little home.

She nodded. "Ready as I'll ever be."

I̲N̲ ̲T̲H̲E̲ ̲T̲E̲L̲ ̲A̲V̲I̲V̲ military bunker's cafeteria, Wu Ying had just carried his plastic dinner tray to a table and sat down, when his world bucked out of control.

The tile floor undulated, rolling in waves under his chair.

The lights, suspended over the dining tables, swung like pendulums.

He clutched the edge of the table as three dinner trays slid toward him. Uniformed men seated at his table grabbed for the plastic trays before they careened into Wu Ying.

His chair rode the wave of the rolling floor, rising and falling, then rising again in a way sure to create motion sickness in any man who was not an experienced sailor.

Nausea lifted Wu Ying's stomach, and he was glad he had not yet eaten. He probably would have lost his dinner.

Shouting filled the cafeteria as the intelligence officers rose and scrambled for the door, some losing their footing on the swelling and receding floor.

Wu Ying stood cautiously and followed them.

He did not wish to remain underground during an earthquake. Having lived through several earthquakes in China, he did not want to die in this one in Israel.

He joined the crowd rushing into the corridor and up a flight of stairs.

No one moved to stop him.

Moments later, he hurried out the exit doors and crossed a sidewalk onto a rolling, heaving, well-manicured lawn.

If he had been detained in the bunker, he had escaped just like that.

He was a free man once again.

Of course, most of his belongings were down in his resident quarters. He patted his pockets. He had his wallet, cell phone, keys, and a few coins. His passport, electronics, and other items remained down in the bunker.

Perhaps he could run down and retrieve them, then join the remaining personnel still exiting the building.

No.

There was no way he would return to an underground location during an earthquake which seemed to be growing worse, rather than stopping.

It should be over by now, but a great jolt threw several officers off balance. One man fell into Wu Ying, sending both tumbling to the ground.

Beneath them, the earth rolled and sighed, then gave a great groan as if it were distressed, followed by a massive upheaval.

Wu Ying's stomach threatened to follow suit, but fortunately, it was still empty.

He crawled toward the center of the lawn, far from any walls that might collapse and fall on him. It was a good place to wait out this quake and its aftershocks.

He sat down and tried to calm the nausea rising in his throat.

Car alarms, set off by the bouncing parking lots, shrieked and wailed.

Emergency alarms on the military facility added to the din as the ground swelled, rolled, and bucked beneath Wu Ying.

He closed his eyes and quickly prayed for Wei Min and Christian in their apartment building. He had no idea whether buildings here were constructed to a strong code for earthquakes. In fact, he didn't know whether quakes were common to this region.

This one shook like the wrath of God, refusing to quit.

In fact... he blinked, trying to remember that passage in

Ezekiel's prophecy. Did it not say something about a great earthquake?

He felt certain it did, but could not recall the exact words. As soon as the earth stopped rolling, he would have to look it up.

Meanwhile, he sat still, trying to settle his nerves and his stomach.

21

Pain tore through Ivan's legs and back, but the terror wouldn't stop. As screams rose in the bunker, the room bucked again, sending men and desks into the air before letting them crash down into each other.

The lights flickered, then went out.

Ivan's world was plunged into black chaos.

Another jolt sent men and furniture crashing into the far wall.

Something hard and sharp smashed into his chest, too near his recent heart surgery scar. Pain screamed through his lungs.

In the deafening blackness, he gingerly touched his chest, expecting it to be caved in. At the end of his bypass surgery, the doctors had wired his ribcage together at his sternum. These thin loops of wire were supposed to hold his chest together for the remainder of his life, since the cartilage would not heal or mend.

His chest structure felt normal as his fingers brushed over it, but his momentary relief was overcome by the pain radiating from the rest of his body.

Ivan hurt all over – legs, hip, back, chest.

This is what it must feel like to be struck by an automobile.

He inhaled, and even that was painful.

Around him, colleagues cried out in the dark room. He thought he heard Pavlov's voice, but he did not hear President Abramov's.

Had anyone been killed?

That was certainly likely.

"Was that a nuclear bomb?" Someone to his left voiced Ivan's worst fear.

Another man moaned, then wailed, "We're all going to die!"

Whatever it was, it had stopped. Or at least, the bunker had stopped bucking and jerking.

"Where are the emergency lights?" Ivan asked.

Normally, modern buildings were equipped with lights indicating exits when the power went out.

"The EMP zapped them!" Irritation and terror laced someone's answer.

Ivan choked on something that tasted like plaster dust.

His colleague was right. If Israel had hit this bunker with a nuclear weapon, the detonation would have created an electromagnetic pulse that would have destroyed any electronic devices that were not specifically hardened to withstand an EMP.

Pain zigged and zagged through his body.

He coughed again, spitting out plaster dust along with something wet and salty.

Was that blood?

Was he bleeding in his lungs and coughing up blood?

He gathered his legs beneath him and attempted to stand up. After bashing into something with his knee, he managed to get to his feet.

Now, if he could find his way to the door... there was no way to know which direction it was. Grit irritated his eyes as he blinked, searching for any light in the darkness.

This place felt like a tomb, and he did not wish to spend his last moments here.

Ignoring the cries of his compatriots, he shuffled forward, hands out in front of him to find obstacles before his shins found them. Eventually, he would come to a wall. From there, he would feel his way around until he came to the door.

As THEY WALKED down the gravel road toward Hideaway, Austin held Sierra's hand in a gentle grip.

"You're awfully quiet," he noted.

"Just thinking." She turned those pretty eyes on him. "You'll be busy once your family gets here."

"*If* they get here," he clarified.

"You think they'll arrive today?"

"I hope so. If they're on the transport, I won't need to wonder where they are or what happened – why they didn't check in this morning." He glanced at her. "And that would also solve the dilemma about my moving to Bolivia. If they're here, I won't be going there."

She smiled. "I like that."

"So do I." He squeezed her hand.

They fell silent for a while, then he said, "I wonder what the newcomers will be like. Old or young? Urban or rural?"

"Maybe a mix of all that," Sierra said. "As long as they're decent, they'll find a way to fit in. I'm concerned that there might be some bad apples in the group."

"I guess we'll need to introduce them to Patmosa's new rules right away," he responded.

In the aftermath of the collapse of the United States, the island had experienced a brief crime boom. That was quickly curtailed when the islanders gathered and approved a set of ordinances with very stiff penalties for crime. Theft, for example, was punishable by death because it could result in the starvation of the victim.

No one had been executed under the new rules yet, but crime had drastically diminished.

"Yeah, good point," Sierra agreed. "Maybe the welcoming committee could take care of explaining those rules before the new arrivals get off the dock."

She glanced at him. "You know, nineteen people might not sound like a whole lot, but that's like an immediate population increase of five percent here. And if another twenty arrive next week, and another thirty after that... I have no idea how we'll all survive. Resources are so limited and strained already."

A light breeze lifted her brown hair and blew it across her shoulders. Overhead, the sun managed to peek through the clouds.

"We'll have to pray for the Lord's provision," Austin answered. "Psalm 37, verse 25 says, 'I have been young, and now am old; yet I have not seen the righteous forsaken, nor his descendants begging bread.'"

She gave him an odd look. "Okay, but what about all those Americans who died this summer? Over two hundred million. Some starved to death. You think none of them were righteous?"

"I imagine many were."

He fell silent for a moment. Sierra had a good point.

And this whole pastor business might be beyond his capabilities. Who was he to answer honest objections like that? He prayed silently for wisdom before he continued.

"Let's examine it a little further, though. It doesn't say evil things don't ever befall the righteous. They're persecuted around the world. They die. The Bible also says the rain falls on the just and the unjust – so large-scale events happen to everyone in a region."

He drew a breath and prepared to step into the proverbial mire.

"However, I believe that God gave American Christians a warning to leave in advance of the crisis. If they failed to heed the warning, or decided it didn't apply to them, or decided to stay, then that was their choice and the result of that decision is on them."

"Wʜᴀᴛ?" Sierra stopped walking. That was a terrible thing to say!

She turned, her mouth agape, and stared at Austin. "What warning? What are you talking about?"

He met her gaze. "In Revelation chapter 18, which portrays the fall of the future mystery Babylon, God's people are commanded to leave that terrible place. It says, 'Come out of her, my people, lest you share in her sins, and lest you receive of her plagues.'"

She dropped his hand. "You're shaming the victims."

"No, I'm only pointing out that the order was clearly given, and the consequences for failure were stated. What Christians did or didn't do with that was up to them."

"But how could they have known?" Sierra sucked in a breath. "Did pastors teach this to their congregations? Did everybody in the churches know?"

He shook his head. "Very few, I think. American pastors

were busy telling their congregants that they'd be raptured any moment now. That before things got really bad, they'd be out of there."

"Then how could the Christians be responsible for making the wrong choice? For staying in America?"

Austin crossed his arms. "They have Bibles, don't they?"

"I guess." She even had one, before she became a believer.

He leaned closer. "They have God's word, Sierra. In their hands! That wasn't possible before the invention of the printing press, but now nearly every Christian in the world has access to a copy."

She frowned.

"So... why didn't they leave, then?" Before he could answer, she faced him directly. "Why didn't you leave? You're on a remote island in Alaska, but that's still Mystery Babylon, isn't it?"

He nodded. "Absolutely. You're right. And I considered leaving, very seriously. When Bella and I were engaged, we discussed where we might go."

Austin got a faraway look in his eyes as he glanced at the forest beyond Sierra. "Anyway, after she died, I didn't care too much anymore. Whether I lived or died. For a while. So I lived my quiet hermit life at the edge of the island and stopped thinking about it."

He turned back to her. "But many believers took the scripture seriously. They did leave the United States."

She was surprised to hear that. "Where did they go?"

"All kinds of places. Mexico, Europe, Africa, South America." He reached for her hand. "We should keep walking."

She fell into step beside him as he continued. "The thing was, at the time, there was no better place to live than the United States. No place had more liberty or freedom. Every country was moving toward totalitarianism, but the U.S. was getting there slower than the others."

Austin kicked at a fir cone on the gravel road. "So it was a difficult decision. They had to leave a country they knew, to go to one that they were sure would be worse – at least in the immediate future."

He glanced at her. "Now, though, they're probably feeling pretty good about wherever they are, in comparison to the country they left behind."

"Yeah, anywhere is better than America now," she agreed.

"But before the war and tsunami, America appeared to be the last best place in the world. So it took a lot of faith to pack up and move away." He squeezed her hand. "It kind of reminds me of Abraham."

She looked up into his dark eyes. "How's that?"

"God told him to leave his country and go to a place that the Lord would show him. If you think moving to a new country now is challenging, imagine doing it without cars or planes or moving vans. But he packed up and headed out. At 75 years old!"

"Wow." Sierra knew a little of the story of Abraham's travels, but she hadn't realized he was so old when he started out. "That's impressive."

"That's Abraham. Patriarch of the Jews, and also the Arabs." He suddenly stopped walking. "We should pray for Israel. They need God's help right now."

IN TEL AVIV, the earthquake finally stopped, but Wu Ying sat silently on the lawn, expecting another jolt. These quakes were often followed by aftershocks, and he was safest on the lawn. Around him, Aman officers helped each other to their feet and checked themselves for injuries.

A female officer looked at Wu Ying and spoke in Hebrew.

He gave her a faint smile and a shrug. "English?"

"Are you alright?" Her gaze scanned him from head to toe. "What are you doing here?"

"I think I am fine. I'm waiting to see if there is an aftershock."

"But what are you doing here, on this base?" Her tone was even, but firm. Strangers and foreigners were not expected to be present on a military base, particularly during a time of war.

"I am assisting the intelligence officers," he answered.

Her brown eyes narrowed. "With whom are you working?"

"Lieutenant Colonel Isaac Meir."

"And your name?"

"Mao Wu Ying."

The woman's gaze carried a great deal of suspicion. He could understand that. She would not know why a Chinese national would be needed during a war with Russia and regional allies. China had no involvement in this war.

"Are you staying on base?" The woman asked.

"Yes."

"Why?"

"I do not know if I can tell you that," he hedged.

"Fine. Come with me. We will get this sorted out." Her tone left no room for argument, so Wu Ying cautiously rose to his feet and joined her as she strode toward the nearest building, which was the one where he had been staying.

"I don't think it's safe to enter a building," he said when it appeared that was exactly what she intended to do.

"The quake is over. You'll be fine." Her hand rested lightly on the holster on her hip.

Seeing few options, he prayed she was right, then entered the building's lobby, where staff had already begun cleaning up the mess. Several employed brooms to sweep up broken window glass, while others replaced items that had fallen from shelves and desks.

His escort approached the security screener. Gesturing to Wu Ying, she asked the officer, "Did you process this man through security today?"

He eyed Wu Ying. "I did. He's staying here at the request of Lieutenant Colonel Meir."

"Thank you." She looked slightly surprised.

Turning to Wu Ying, she said, "I'll escort you to your room. Where are you staying?"

"I'm not comfortable being underground until we are past the possibility of aftershocks."

Her mouth curved downward. "I am not concerned much with your comfort, Mister Mao. We are prosecuting a war, and I need to return to my duties. However, I cannot allow you to roam free at this facility."

The security officer stepped up to intervene. "I'll contact the lieutenant colonel and get instructions. Meanwhile, you can leave our guest here with me."

"Thank you." She gave him a grateful smile, then hustled out the door.

The security screener focused on Wu Ying and gestured to a nearby bench. "Please take a seat. Someone will be with you soon."

He did as he was told, and saw the security officer make a quick phone call. A minute later, a young soldier approached.

"Mao Wu Ying?"

"Yes." He rose from the bench.

"Please come with me."

The man escorted him directly to Lieutenant Colonel

Meir's office, where several staff were organizing the earth-quake-disrupted room.

The senior officer eyed him. "I was told you did not wish to return to your underground quarters due to concerns about a possible aftershock."

"Yes."

"I understand. Please have a seat."

Wu Ying took one of the guest chairs, while the staff swirled around him, putting the office back in order.

"It was quite a quake," he ventured.

"Indeed," Meir agreed, picking papers off the floor. "They had it much worse at the northern front."

"Was that the epicenter?"

"It was." Meir assisted a man who was re-orienting his desk, which had turned sideways in the small office. "Would you believe it registered 9.6 on the Richter scale?"

"No." Wu Ying's jaw slacked. "Did it really?"

"Yes, it did. So it wasn't bad here at all. But at the front, it's a terrible mess."

"Oh! That reminds me." Wu Ying paused to consider what he was going to say, but then plunged on. "Do you happen to have access to a Bible? Or your scriptures, which we call the Old Testament? There is a passage in Ezekiel that I must look at."

Meir rubbed his forehead. "Now? Why?"

"Because –" he leaned forward. "I think it pertains to this exact war, and it prophesies a great earthquake in Israel. I want to see what else it reveals. Are you familiar with the text?"

"No. I am not a religious man."

"Neither was I, until very recently." Wu Ying held the man's gaze. "I could read it online, if I could have access to a computer. Or I could retrieve my Bible from my quarters."

"I thought you were afraid to be underground?"

"It will only take a minute."

Meir huffed a sigh, then turned to one of the soldiers who was straightening the books on his shelf. "Please go to Mister Mao's room and bring back his Bible."

22

Shuffling hesitantly in the completely dark bunker, Ivan felt ahead with his hands. He maneuvered around the corner of an overturned table, and then touched something vertical, flat and solid. Feeling quickly for corners or edges, he found none. It was a wall!

A moment later, an eerie glow cast the palest light into the bunker. Ivan turned to focus on the source.

Someone had found their cell phone, and it still worked!

As a cheer rose in the room, relief flooded his heart.

A functional cell phone indicated that the bunker had not been nuked. A nuclear explosion would have destroyed electronic circuitry with an EMP, while a conventional weapon would not.

Moments later, another phone glowed, and then a third.

Ivan would not die of radiation sickness after all!

He reached for his own cell phone, then remembered he had left it at his computer workstation. Now it was lost in the debris of the room.

He cursed himself for failing to keep his phone on his person, then added a second curse for being too panicked to think logically earlier and ask if anyone else had their phone on them.

Now, aided by the pale glow of several phones, he felt his way quickly along the wall. As the men turned on their phones' flashlights, shafts of light cut through the room.

Clouds of plaster dust made the air appear foggy and taste gritty.

As one beam of light swung across the bunker, Ivan spotted the exit door and carefully made his way to it.

He expected to find a collapsed corridor, but when he opened the door, the hallway was clear. And it had emergency illumination.

"Come on," he called to his colleagues. "Let's get out of this death trap!"

"Help me." The weak cry came from his left.

A table pinned Pavlov to the wall.

Ignoring his urge to rush away from the unstable carnage, Ivan turned back to help the old general. Another man assisted him in getting the table off Pavlov's legs.

"Can you stand?" Ivan asked.

"Perhaps," he wheezed. "Give me a hand."

Ivan extended both hands to the senior military leader, while the other man slid an arm behind Pavlov to boost him up. Together, they got Pavlov onto his shaky legs.

"Put your arm around my shoulders." Ivan wrapped his arm around Pavlov's waist, letting the old man lean against him. "Let's go."

They stepped out the door, following other men into the hall.

"There should be stairs," Ivan said, looking for them. "Where are they?"

"We came down an elevator," Pavlov wheezed.

"Well, I do not think we will be going up that way," Ivan objected.

"This way," a man shouted. "I've found stairs around the corner!"

Ivan pulled Pavlov forward, limping to the corner, where he found the door to the stairwell propped open. Remarkably, the sturdy metal stairs appeared to be intact.

Pavlov groaned. "Get me out of here."

"You're going to have to climb, my friend," Ivan said. "Summon your courage."

Men shuffled past them as they began their slow climb up the steps.

After the longest time that might have only been two minutes, Ivan emerged from the stairwell and was greeted by the sights and sounds of war.

STANDING on the narrow road to Hideaway, Austin gripped Sierra's hand and prayed earnestly for Israel. When he finished, he smiled at her.

"I know God's going to work on their behalf. It's going to be amazing."

"I'm sure you're right," she agreed. "Meanwhile, we'd better hurry to get down to the dock. The transport is due in less than half an hour."

He glanced at his watch. "Oh, boy. Yeah, we better step it up."

They hurried down the tree-lined gravel road, past the cemetery and the mayor's sawmill. Making good time, they soon arrived at the outskirts of Hideaway, where the road turned to pavement and the tsunami damage was the most apparent.

While some buildings clung to their original foundations, others leaned listlessly to the side. Many had been washed away entirely.

"It makes me sad every time I come down here," Sierra said. "My hometown. Where I grew up. Such a wreck!"

Austin wasn't sure what to say to that, so he wrapped an arm around her shoulder. "I'm sorry. It's awful."

A grey haze rose from the chimney of the smokehouse, where someone was smoking fish caught in the tempestuous waters of the Inside Passage earlier in the day. The cannery stood silent beside it.

Had the community run out of jars or lids? Austin knew that would happen sooner or later. When they couldn't can anymore, maybe they could pickle the fish. It seemed like some old Europeans did that. Not that he'd be terribly excited about pickled fish.

Fresh or smoked were fine with him. Dried fish might be okay. Once some of the islanders constructed a salt works to collect salt from the briny Pacific, they would be able to have salted fish. And many other salty foods.

"Look!" Sierra yanked on his arm. She pointed out beyond the marina. "The transport boat!"

He followed her gaze. Sure enough, a sleek vessel moved cleanly through the water, headed straight toward Hideaway with its one repaired dock.

"It's weird," she said, "but I'm kind of excited. Maybe we'll get some great new neighbors."

"Good." He rubbed his eyebrow. "I hope so."

He was glad she felt enthusiastic, even if it was momentary. He could only imagine how these new transplants were feeling.

They'd survived the war and all the horrors that followed, made their way into Canada, and were being thrust out onto a tiny, remote Alaskan island, likely against their will. Presumably, they'd planned to live in Canada, which presented a culture generally familiar to them, and wasn't totally destroyed. But Canada ejected them, and here they were.

He imagined they were angry or scared. Or both.

So Sierra's welcoming greeting would lighten their burdens. At least until she approached with a tongue depressor and told them to open their mouths and say "Ahhhh."

Would his cousins be on board?

Most likely.

He certainly hoped so.

While it would be challenging to accommodate them and their special needs, he expected they would be relieved to be welcomed by a family member, and they'd be done with their treacherous, slow travels.

For his part, he would be glad to know they were okay, and he'd be able to check on them and help them get established here on the island.

The boat was still too far away to make out the features of individual travelers, but he kept scanning. Surely they would be there!

SIERRA WATCHED AUSTIN, then the approaching vessel, then Austin again. His jaw muscles worked as his keen eyes studied the boat.

Was he nervous? Worried?

Their friends and neighbors gathered on the beach, then walked out on the dock. She glanced at the group. The mayor was here, along with Laszlo Koval and Jim Jenkins, both elders from Fellowship Farm, plus Daisy and her husband Timothy, Grandma and a few others.

She watched the boat as it drew near. It looked similar to the high-speed Alaska ferries. Not the big ones that carried cargo and vehicles, but the sleek, passenger-only boats.

A dozen or more people stood near the bow of the boat, no doubt surveilling their new home and the welcoming party that gathered there.

What were they thinking? It must be jarring to be evicted from Canadian civilization and tossed out on the Hideaway beach, like Jonah was tossed out by the great fish.

They didn't have any homes here, or any prospect of homes. No vehicles, no jobs, no food.

It was crazy, really.

And these folks had landed at a civilized island with kind people who weren't actually starving to death. What about the other folks, who landed on other Alaskan islands where they'd be met by starving, hostile locals?

That would be terrifying.

As the boat drew near, she lifted an arm in a high, friendly wave.

"Hello!" She raised her voice to echo out over the water.

Several people at the prow raised their hands and waved back at her.

She turned to Austin and grinned. "Do you see your family?"

He stared, then blinked and stared some more. "I'm not sure. I don't see anybody that definitely looks like them."

"They might be inside. It's breezy out on the deck."

"Yeah." He sounded uncertain. "Maybe you're right."

Sierra clasped her hands together. She was surprised she'd developed some enthusiasm for welcoming these strangers to her island. Perhaps it was foolish – they might be the death of them all. But still, she believed it was better to offer hospitality rather than hostility. These folks had not chosen to be here. They wanted to live in Canada.

But now they were here, and everyone would have to make the best of it.

Hopefully, Austin's family would be on board. Dealing with a schizophrenic was a scary proposition, since the islanders had no meds to level out the psychosis. They might need to isolate or detain him when he was headed into a bad cycle.

But she felt eager to meet Austin's grandfather and cousins. What would they be like? Would they like her?

She glanced at Austin. His jaw looked tense. She turned her gaze back to the incoming boat. "Still don't see them?"

He shook his head. "Nope."

IN HIS HANDLER'S OFFICE, Wu Ying waited impatiently for the assistant to return with his Bible. Finally, the man returned and handed him the book. "I was not expecting it to have a science fiction cover."

Wu Ying smiled and held the book aloft. "In China, I had to disguise it from the communists. In an underground bunker's restroom, I used chewing gum to attach this novel's cover to it during the war."

Lieutenant Colonel Isaac Meir gave him a thoughtful glance. "You must have many stories, having lived your entire life in communism."

"Not many good ones, sadly." Wu Ying flipped the Bible open. "I kept the science fiction cover on my Bible to remind me where I came from. And I read the Bible daily to remind me where I'm going."

No one responded, so he turned to Ezekiel and found chapter 38. He began reading aloud in verse 19.

"For in My jealousy and in the fire of My wrath I have spoken: 'Surely in that day there shall be a great earthquake in the land of Israel, so that the fish of the sea, the birds of the heavens, the beasts of the field, all creeping things that creep on the earth, and all men who are on the face of the earth shall shake at My presence. The mountains shall be thrown down, the steep places shall fall, and every wall shall fall to the ground.'"

He looked up. "This passage speaks, I believe, of the war you are currently waging. The Lord God comes and fights on behalf of Israel. The earthquake is part of God's wrath."

Meir shook his head. "Sorry, I don't buy it. The earthquake, like so many recent natural disasters, is due to climate change. If people don't start taking better care of the earth, it's going to get very difficult to sustain life here."

Wu Ying nearly laughed out loud, until he noticed Meir's face.

The man was totally serious.

He truly believed what he was saying.

Wu Ying reined in his mirth and took a different tack.

"What you call 'climate change,' is what the Bible describes will happen at the end of the world. It's end times weather and disasters. Earthquakes in various places, droughts, plagues...." He fixed his gaze on his handler. "Did you know the Bible says it will get so hot, the sun will burn people, and also there won't be rain for three and a half years?"

"That's ludicrous!" Meir straightened his lapel.

"Not necessarily," he countered. "Your own history recounts that the same thing happened in the past. Which

Jewish prophet was it? Elijah? He prayed, and it did not rain for three years and six months."

Meir huffed a sigh. "Please. I've heard that tale. It's just a fable."

Wu Ying closed his mouth. Clearly, this man was not ready to hear the truth. Perhaps some day, he would be open to the Lord. Until then, there was no point in arguing with him. But Meir had just stepped up to the top of Wu Ying's prayer list.

As he emerged from the devastated bunker, Ivan was blinded by the setting sun. His eyes had grown accustomed to the dim emergency illumination in the bunker hallway and stairwell, and now a brilliant sunset blazed into his retinas.

He ducked his head and averted his eyes.

Pavlov, still leaning against him, cursed. He pointed to a concrete vehicle barrier. "Get me over there, so I can sit down."

Alarms and sirens blared through Syria's capital city as missiles screamed overhead. The acrid stench of smoke competed with the dust of war's destruction.

Ivan coughed as he helped the old man to the traffic barrier.

Pavlov eased back against it. "I should have retired yesterday."

"And missed all this?" Ivan asked, letting the sarcasm drip.

The old man blinked up at him, then coughed a raucous laugh.

Turning grim, Ivan watched his colleagues and foreign

compatriots emerge from the bunker's stairwell. "How are we going to monitor the war now?"

"A backup location, I'm sure," Pavlov responded.

Ivan surveyed the scene at the bunker. He could not see where the bomb had hit. There was no blast site. No detonation damage.

"Pavlov. I don't think we were bombed."

"Bombed?" The old man coughed another laugh. "No, my man. That was no bomb. It was an earthquake!"

"Was it?" Ivan turned to see if Pavlov was serious. He had never felt an earthquake before.

Then, as if to validate the old warrior's words, the ground shifted beneath his feet, then rocked and jolted, and Ivan was tossed to the ground.

The quake went on forever.

Seconds passed as the earth quivered and bucked, then minutes, and what felt like hours. But it could not be hours, because the sun was still setting.

Wails and shouts filled the air. Every car alarm in the city of Damascus blared.

Meanwhile, air-raid sirens screamed continuously, warning citizens to get under cover.

There was no place to go.

Pinning his hands against his ears, Ivan scrambled to Pavlov's concrete vehicle barrier, where he hunkered down, waiting for the world to stop shaking and shrieking.

A terrifying noise roared behind him, and he turned in time to see an entire apartment building collapse. Behind it, a skyscraper swayed, then leaned at a horrifying angle before it fell across at least five city blocks.

Still the earth continued heaving and shaking.

Dust and debris filled the air and Ivan's lungs. Grit stung his eyes.

Two blocks away, a small explosion resulted in a deafening boom and then a massive fire broke out on the military complex.

Had a gas line had been hit?

Beside him, Pavlov coughed and wheezed. "Have you seen the president?"

"No." Ivan blinked, trying to clear his dry, scratchy eyes. "Not since this all began."

"Don't you think we should try to find him? Help him get out of the bunker?"

Of course Pavlov did not mean "we," as in both of them. The old man was in no shape to return down those stairs. He was saying Ivan should do it. Perhaps he was right, but Ivan had no desire to re-enter that death trap.

As if to confirm his decision, the ground lurched and bucked again, tossing him hard against the concrete barrier.

On Hideaway's dock, Austin stood and watched the boat as it eased into the marina. The engines reduced power, and the prow turned to align with the dock. He could make out faces on the deck now, and did not see a familiar one among them.

Where was his family?

As Sierra mentioned, they might be inside the boat, staying out of the cool, breezy air. Grandpa should be doing that, for his health. But Austin expected his cousins to stand on the deck, checking out their new home and looking for him.

Minutes ticked by as the crew secured the boat and lowered the gangplank.

Led by the mayor, Austin's friends and neighbors moved forward on the dock to meet the newcomers. He remained behind, watching each person as they made their way down the gangplank. Many carried some kind of luggage, or toted backpacks.

Most likely, those bags carried everything they still owned in the world.

These people were far worse off than he was. Even when the mega-tsunami destroyed his home, he still had the pickup he'd left parked at Fellowship Farm with some belongings in it. Plus, he had friends and neighbors who helped him get back on his feet.

These folks had nothing but a few bags of clothing and despair.

Fifteen people disembarked.

The other four expected passengers, his family members, apparently had not made the trip.

"Welcome to Hideaway, everyone!" The mayor's voice boomed over the small crowd. "I'm Mayor Jake Williams. Like most towns in Southeast Alaska, Hideaway was destroyed by the mega-tsunami. Most of us live higher on the island now."

He smiled magnanimously. "Before you decide whether you want to remain here, there are three things you should know. First, you'll undergo a health check. Second, you'll be quarantined for ten days."

The newcomers began objecting, but he raised a hand and continued. "It's necessary for our protection and yours. And third, we have very stringent laws here on the island. Criminal punishments are swift and severe. So if you have any thought of theft or violence or anything like that, or if you don't want to submit to a health exam and quarantine, you should get right back on that boat."

He pointed at the still-lowered gangplank.

The muttering voices ceased. Apparently, there were worse things than strict prosecution of crime. These people had likely experienced some crime or violence over the past few months.

Austin expected the captain or crew to protest the idea of any of these passengers re-boarding the boat, but they stood by in silence.

"Very well, then," Mayor Williams said. "Those who are willing to abide by these requirements are welcome to stay."

The mayor turned to Sierra and motioned toward her. "This is Sierra Forrester, our medical manager. She'll be conducting your health exams, along with her assistants."

Then the mayor turned to Laszlo and Jim. "These gentlemen are Laszlo Koval and Jim Jenkins, elders of the religious community that will be hosting you during your quarantine. If any of you objects to staying in a religious institution, you might want to get back on the boat."

Not a single voice raised an objection.

Austin made his way toward a crew member and spoke quietly. "We were expecting nineteen people on this transport. I only count fifteen. Do you know what happened to the others?"

The swarthy man shook his head. "No, but you could ask the captain. He's up there, by the top of the gangplank."

"Thanks." Austin started up the ramp.

SIERRA WATCHED Austin head up the gangplank, but the mayor distracted her with a question.

"Sierra, where do you want to conduct the medical exams?"

She turned to him. "I can conduct preliminary exams in the cannery, since it's not in operation today. Then later I can do follow-ups at the quarantine building, if necessary."

"Very well." He turned to the newcomers. "Please follow Sierra. She'll get you all started."

Laszlo stepped forward. "It might be a good idea to set up three stations – health, laws and general information. We can rotate people through in small groups. That way, they get their medical exam done, plus learn about our new laws and penalties, and also learn about Patmosa Island and what we do here."

"Great idea." The mayor nodded. "Let's have you all divide into three groups, about five people each, and go from there."

The locals offered to help carry luggage off the dock to the beach, where the newcomers split up into groups. One family of six remained together, as did a family of five, leaving four singles in the final group.

Laszlo gave everyone a disarming smile. "I'll do the short course on our laws and penalties, and maybe Jim could do an overview of the island and the situation here?"

Jim Jenkins tugged on his white beard. "Sure. Happy to. Group One, come this way, and I'll tell you what Patmosa is all about these days."

The larger family moved in his direction.

"Okay, Group Two, step over here, and I'll tell you about our laws and expectations," Laszlo said.

Sierra smiled at the four singles.

"I guess you're Group Three. Follow me to the cannery building." She pointed it out. "My grandma and Daisy Hemburg will be assisting me with your medical checks."

She turned and led the way, glancing out at the boat as she walked. Austin was still out there, apparently speaking to the captain or crew.

Daisy's husband Tim fell in step with her as she approached the door. "Thought you might need an extra hand," he said.

Sierra noted the gun on his hip. "Sure. That'd be great."

She didn't really expect any trouble, but was happy to know it would be quashed if it came her way.

Inside the cannery, she turned on the LED lights that were powered by a single solar panel mounted on the building's south wall.

"Okay, everyone." She smiled at the strangers. "We'll make this as painless as possible. I'm sorry we don't have chairs, but the wait should be short."

Pulling the clipboard, paper and pens from her pack, she handed a few extra sheets of paper to Daisy and Tim. "It'd be great if you could start getting background health info, while I begin the physical exams."

Then she handed the clipboard to Grandma. "And if you could write each person's name and age at the top, and then make a note of each thing I tell you as I work…?"

"You got it." Grandma took a pen and the clipboard, and turned to the nearest newcomer. "Name and age, please."

As a massive aftershock rocked Tel Aviv, Wu Ying and Lieutenant Colonel Meir huddled in Meir's office with several members of the intelligence staff. The building swayed and shuddered.

"Find cover," Meir shouted. "Brace yourselves!"

He ducked under his desk.

Clutching his Bible under his arm, Wu Ying moved to the doorway.

The building moaned and heaved.

"We have to get out of here," Wu Ying yelled. "Now!"

As Meir and his staff hurried toward him, Wu Ying fled down the corridor. He entered the stairwell and took the steps two at a time, lurching into the wall as the building rocked.

He prayed as he ran. "Please God, get us out!"

Time seemed to slow as he reached the lower landing and saw the exit door. He threw his weight against the crash bar, flinging it open.

Stopping outside, he held the door open for the others. "Hurry, hurry!"

Meir was the last one out, and they ran toward the rolling, heaving lawn. Sirens wailed and people screamed.

The ground gave a vicious lurch, and Wu Ying fell sideways.

Behind him, a massive boom followed a terrible cracking sound. He turned in time to see the building he had left moments earlier crashing into a heap of rubble.

Dust and debris filled the air and his lungs.

If he had remained in that building for one more minute, he would be dead.

He thanked God for his life, then waited for the rolling to stop.

But the aftershock was not finished.

Around Wu Ying, other buildings shook violently. The earth ripped them from their foundations and toppled them to the ground.

Shrieks filled his ears.

Panic filled the screams of the injured and terrified.

Wu Ying prayed for the crisis and carnage to end.

If it was this bad in Tel Aviv, he could only imagine what was happening at the epicenter. He had never seen such a powerful earthquake in his life.

This was a biblical quake, and he had little doubt God had done it, just as He had said.

24

In Damascus, Ivan cowered beside the concrete traffic barrier. Beneath him, the ground rolled and shook. Overhead, Israel's missiles screamed until reaching their destinations, pounding the city with violence and destruction.

He kept his hands pinned to his ears, and closed his gritty eyes.

Every breath he took was filled with smoke and with dust from buildings collapsed by the earthquake or blown up by the bombs.

Finally, after half a lifetime, the ground stopped heaving.

Ivan opened his eyes. Pavlov hunkered inches from him, his old eyes red from the smoky grit. They watered and dripped along the sides of his nose.

Pavlov's hand shot out and gripped Ivan's arm. "We're alive!"

"For now," Ivan agreed.

A missile shrieked overhead, then slammed into a building at the far end of the military complex.

He focused on Pavlov. "We've got to get out of here."

"Sure," the old man agreed. "Lead the way."

Being unfamiliar with this base and with the city, Ivan had no idea where to go. He looked around for a knowledgeable person, but everyone had scrambled like rats for perceived safety.

As he scanned the area, darkness fell across the city. He looked over his shoulder. The sunset had been spectacular, but it was not normal for daylight to end suddenly on a clear, sunny day like this.

A massive dark cloud rose ominously from the west.

For a moment, he thought it might be a mushroom cloud. Had someone authorized nuclear weapons?

But then he realized the shape was not truly a mushroom, and it was expanding far too widely for that. It grew at an exponential pace, blotting out the setting sun until the land was nearly dark – in the space of a few seconds.

As the cloud reached Damascus, it began raining. Not a light sprinkle or a steady drip, but a massive outpouring.

Ivan was instantly soaked, from his hair to his socks.

"Let's find shelter," Pavlov wheezed.

Grabbing the old man's arm, Ivan helped him to his feet and pulled him toward a building with an overhang that would normally shelter the windows from the desert sun.

Hail began to fall when the men were within a few meters of the sturdy overhang.

Ivan had never seen such hail. It was larger than hen's eggs. It struck the ground, bounced, and fell again.

He slipped on it, falling to the soaked pavement with Pavlov.

As the big balls of ice struck their shoulders and backs, they scrambled on hands and knees for the shelter of the building's overhang.

Finally reaching shelter, Pavlov leaned his back against the building. His hands and arms shook.

Ivan shivered from the soaking rain and the astonishing hail. He turned to the old general.

"Have you ever –"

"No." Water dripped from Pavlov's jaws. "I have never seen anything like this. Earthquake, rain and hail?"

The old man blinked rain out of his eyes. "It is an act of God."

Ivan did not believe in such things. He did not think Pavlov did, either. Still, this circumstance was inexplicable. How could all these things happen at once?

And why did it have to be on the day of their great invasion?

Or maybe... it was *because* of their invasion.

It was difficult to not wonder about that.

As he pressed his cold, rain-soaked back against the hard concrete wall, the hailstones grew larger. They had been the size of eggs, but they increased to the size of baseballs, and then softballs.

Anyone who was struck in the head by one would surely be killed.

In the parking area, hailstones pounded vehicles, smashing the windows and hammering the fiberglass.

Meanwhile, rain dumped continuously from the heavens at the same time, flooding the military installation until the hail was floating on the water that rushed toward drains that were far from adequate for this deluge.

Water rose, filling the parking areas.

In his childhood, Ivan had heard the story of Noah and the flood. It must have been something like this.

He could barely see the scene before him now, with the black cloud overhead casting the world in an unearthly darkness. But he heard the massive hail pounding the ground and the floodwater.

It sounded like the roar of a thousand drums.

ON THE SHIP'S DECK, Austin met with the captain. He introduced himself and asked about the missing passengers.

"Why do you care?" The man eyed him warily. "Thought you'd be happy to have fewer vagabonds dumped on your island."

"They're my family," he explained. "My cousins and my grandfather."

"Are they now?" The captain rubbed his short beard. "What'd you say your last name was?"

"Martin. Austin Martin. I'm the pastor here." As if that would expedite anything. Preachers and churches were held in low regard these days.

"A pastor, eh?" White eyebrows rose over surprised blue eyes. "You still have a church going?"

"Of course. Everyone has spiritual needs," he said. "Whether or not they know it."

"And that's how you make your living?" His tone carried a challenge.

"No." Austin shook his head. "Before the war, I was a novelist. And now... well, we all pull on the oars together, so to speak."

He did not want to mention the farm to a man like this one, who would be traveling far and talking to many people.

The captain eyed him. "You're trim, but none of you appear to be starving. I hope you haven't resorted to cannibalism."

Austin's jaw dropped. "What? Are people doing that?"

A grim nod provided the answer he didn't want to hear.

He stared at the captain until he was convinced the man meant it.

God's curses for disobedience outlined in Deuteronomy chapter 28, including starvation leading to cannibalism, flashed through his mind.

"That's horrible."

"Yes. And that's not the worst of it, either."

"Don't say any more. I don't want to know. Unless...."

Horror flooded through Austin.

"Is that what happened? To my family?"

IN THE CANNERY BUILDING, Sierra processed the newcomers as quickly and thoroughly as she could. Grandma took notes and checked for lice. Daisy chatted up everyone while inspecting their belongings for bedbugs.

Thankfully, no one found any lice, nits or bedbugs.

An even bigger relief was that she didn't discover any fevers, and no one reported any recent diarrhea.

As she worked, she tried to get to know a little about each person.

The last, and eldest, newcomer was Jason Tredwell, 61, and he was the grandfather in the six-member family. His daughter and son-in-law were in their mid-thirties and had three children, aged 8, 10 and 11.

"I was diabetic," Jason said, "but I've been off my meds for a month now, and I think I'm doing okay."

"You're Type 2." Sierra pointed out the obvious. "You've probably lost a good deal of weight, and maybe got more exercise lately?"

"Oh, yeah." He patted his stomach. "I've lost thirty pounds, at least. And I haven't had any sweets lately, and not many carbs."

"What did you do for a living?" She reached for a new tongue depressor, but waited for his answer.

"I was a vet."

"Military veteran?" She eyed him. He didn't seem to have that military bearing that a lot of guys have, even decades after service.

Jason laughed. "Veterinarian. Large animal."

She took a step back and eyed him. "That's great! You'll fit in well here."

"You have some bears or lions you want me to treat?" His brown eyes twinkled.

"We have a farm." It was the first time she'd mentioned it to the newcomers. "And in addition to cows, we could use your expertise for people, as well."

"Ah, no. I don't know anything about humans. Other than being one, of course."

"Open up and say 'Ah.'"

As he did so, she checked his mouth, tonsils and visible throat. "You can suture. You can tie off a bleeding blood vessel. You can give injections."

She tossed the used depressor. "Things aren't like they used to be, Dr. Tredwell. Everyone's skills and experience are put to use here. My cousin is pregnant, and I'll expect you to be present for her delivery when the time comes."

He looked a little surprised, then gave an agreeable nod.

"I'll do whatever I can. Just remember, all the previous births I attended came out with four legs and furry faces."

⁓

AT THE TEL AVIV military facility, Wu Ying had sat on the lawn in the middle of great destruction. He clutched his Bible under his arm. Most of his other belongings were now buried under several stories of rubble. All around him, buildings had collapsed and fallen.

Then, he'd watched in astonishment as an even stranger thing had happened.

When the sun set, a massive cloud had formed to their north, rising in a clear blue sky. It grew expansively over many miles of territory in only a few minutes.

Wu Ying had never seen a larger or darker cloud.

His heart pounded as sirens continued to raise their deafening wails.

Beside him, Lieutenant Colonel Meir made one rapid phone call after another, holding his phone to his right ear and covering his left to block out the deafening noise.

Unfortunately for Wu Ying, he could not understand a word of it, because his handler was speaking in Hebrew. Still, he could hear the consternation in his tone, and see the shock and astonishment on the man's face.

In the distance, booms of thunder rolled across the valley. Not one or two, or even dozens, but hundreds. Every few seconds, fresh thunder signaled new lightning.

Finally, Meir ended his calls. His face looked pale as he turned to Wu Ying, and he wore the strangest expression.

"What else does your Bible say about this war?" His tone was sincere, not mocking as Wu Ying might have expected. "Is there something about a storm?"

"Yes, I believe so." In the twilight, Wu Ying opened the book again to Ezekiel. He ran his finger down the pages as he skimmed the text. "Here it is, in the twenty-second and twenty-third verses of chapter 38."

He read aloud. "'And I will bring him to judgment with

pestilence and bloodshed; I will rain down on him, on his troops, and on the many peoples who are with him, flooding rain, great hailstones, fire, and brimstone. Thus I will magnify Myself and sanctify Myself, and I will be known in the eyes of many nations. Then they shall know that I am the LORD.'"

Meir's eyes widened.

"Can I see that?" He held out his hand.

Wu Ying gave him the Bible.

Meir fell silent as he scanned the scripture. After a while, he closed the book and handed it back to Wu Ying.

"Well." He stared off into the thundering distance. "That about sums up what I'm hearing from the front lines. Intense rain, massive hailstones. It's insane."

Wu Ying struggled to maintain a neutral expression as he considered that news.

If this didn't prompt Meir to re-consider the reality and power of God, he didn't know what would. All these events were prophesied thousands of years ago, and they were happening now, at this very moment.

25

Ivan huddled under the military building's overhang as darkness fell along with the most wicked rain he'd ever witnessed. Then there was the humongous hail. The dark sky was broken frequently by the streaks of Israel's missiles pounding the military base and other Damascus targets, with their resulting explosions and fires.

The cacophony was deafening.

He kept his hands pinned to his ears, but it barely muted the roar of the hail, the screams of people he could not see in the dark, and the shrieks and wails of sirens and car alarms. The explosions were the worst, as they were the most startling. And lethal.

It was only a matter of time before this building, where he and Pavlov had sought shelter from the pounding rain and deadly hail, would be blown up by an Israeli warhead.

When that happened, he would likely die.

Perhaps he would live and be maimed.

Suddenly, lightning split open the night sky, illuminating Ivan's surroundings with garish brilliant whiteness.

In the unpredictable flashes, he saw men on the ground,

floating in the floodwater, apparently beaten to death by the massive hailstones.

In the next moment, thunder rocked his world and deafened him. Hands against his ears were little help against the horrific noise.

Beside him, Pavlov cried out.

Then he cursed.

Ivan gritted his teeth and pressed his back against the building. He'd considered attempting to enter it, but thought better of that.

While going indoors might protect him from the rain and hail, it might also prove to be a death trap when the military building suffered a blow from an Israeli warhead. Or the walls might collapse in an earthquake aftershock.

No, it was better to be outside, under the overhang, then be trapped inside a building.

Lightning flashed again, possibly even closer this time, and it revealed the water rising to the edge of the sidewalk where he sat cowering against the wall. Very soon, the water would overrun the sidewalk and flood his already-drenched feet.

If he was in standing water when lightning touched down – well, there was nothing he could do about that. He'd be a fried man.

"We need to go," Pavlov yelled after the thunder died back. "Get to higher ground!"

"Where?" Ivan had paid attention to his surroundings, and in the darkness again now, he could not recall any better location.

"I'm going inside," the old general hollered.

"The Jews are going to hit this building," Ivan objected.

"It's either that or the lightning," Pavlov shouted. "I'll take my chances with the Jews!"

Cool water seeped into Ivan's boots. The floodwater had obviously risen over the sidewalk. He stood and cursed the storm, the rain, the hail, the lightning.

As if in answer, a brilliant arc of electricity illuminated the stormy sky and zig-zagged toward him.

Ivan raised his fist and screamed.

He should not have moved his hands away from his ears.

The loudest thunder he had ever heard burst his eardrums.

The acrid smell of sulphur – brimstone – filled the air.

He coughed and gagged and covered his injured ears.

Never in his life had he seen such a storm.

He felt sure no one had ever witnessed a storm such as this. Preceded by a terrible earthquake, followed by a monstrous storm cloud arising in moments out of a clear blue sky, darkening the earth with pounding rain and lethal hailstones, together with terrible lightning and deafening thunder... who had ever heard of such a storm?

It could destroy his brilliant military strategy.

The tanks would be bogged down in the floodwaters, the soldiers would be killed by the hail, roads and bridges were no doubt damaged by the earthquake and resulting mudslides, and everything was endangered by the electrical storm.

Pavlov gripped his arm and shouted, but Ivan could not understand him. His ears rang. He stared dumbly at the man's screaming mouth and made out some of the words.

"...inside... now!"

Ivan nodded. He was ready to take his chances inside a building that would soon be flattened by a Jewish missile, rather than wait to be electrocuted by the lightning.

ON THE SHIP'S DECK, Austin's heart thundered in his ears. Was it possible that his family had been the victims of horrendous crime?

Of *cannibalism*?

The captain shook his head. "No, nothing like that."

A huge rush of air escaped Austin's lungs. "But where are they? Do you know why they aren't here?"

"I do." The captain eyed him. "A violent crime committed last night, and your relatives are being detained in Canada."

"Violent crime... my relatives?" Austin stared at the man. "Are you sure?"

"Of course I'm sure." He pulled a cigarette from a pack, then offered one to Austin. "Smoke?"

"No." He struggled to breathe. "What kind of crime?"

"Not sure. I didn't get any details. Just 'violent crime,' that's all I was told." The captain gave him a sympathetic look. "Sorry if I was brusque. I was trying to determine if you might be involved in some crime ring with them."

"What?" Austin stared at the man. "How?"

He shrugged. "I don't know. But you were intent on finding out about them, and they're sitting in jail, so...."

The captain lit his cigarette and inhaled deeply, then blew out the smoke.

"They're in jail." Austin tried to picture his cousins and grandfather in a Canadian jail. It required a huge stretch of his imagination. "Can I get them out? My grandfather is quite old. Do they need bail money?"

"I don't know." He took another puff on the cigarette. "I can give you the name of the jail, and you can follow up."

Austin tried to absorb the shocking news. Tried to figure out what to do about it.

"I'll get that info for you, Pastor," the captain said, "and then I need to be going. I've got three more stops today."

"But...." Austin drew a breath and glanced toward the cannery where Sierra was working on medical exams. Then he turned to the captain.

"Are you going back to Prince Rupert? Can I ride along? I need to help my family."

"That won't work," the older man answered. "I'm under orders not to pick up any new passengers."

Austin momentarily considered stowing away, but had no idea how to do that, and realized he probably shouldn't anyway.

"Alright." He sighed, then met the captain's gaze. "I'd appreciate any information you can give me before you leave."

IN THE CANNERY, Sierra wrapped up her medical exams. She gathered her supplies and re-packed them in her backpack, then headed outside. Her gaze swept the beach and the dock for Austin, and she spotted him coming down the ship's gangplank.

Either he'd had a talk with the captain, or he'd taken a tour of the boat. She'd bet on the first option.

While the newcomers joined her neighbors in lining up for Tom's Taxi, she walked out on the dock to meet Austin.

Tension lined his forehead and darkened his eyes.

"What happened?" She gripped her backpack straps. "What's wrong?"

"My family...." He lowered his voice. "They're in jail!"

"What?" She stared at him. "Why? Where?"

"Some kind of violent crime. In Canada." He pulled a

piece of paper from his hip pocket and unfolded it. "I've got the name of the jail here, and phone number and address...."

A lot of good that would do, without phone service or a functional postal service.

"What are you going to do, Austin?" Worry filled her mind and ebbed into her voice. "Are you going there?"

"I tried to catch a ride on the boat, but no luck." He cast a contemptuous look over his shoulder at the fast ferry. "I'll pray. It could be worse, I guess. In jail, they'll at least get three hots and a cot."

Sierra tried to hide her frown. She'd heard plenty of horror stories about stabbings and other violence in jails and prisons.

"I'll pray, too," she promised.

He reached for her hand. They walked silently toward the beach. At the end of the dock, he looked at her.

"I'm really concerned, Sierra. I don't understand how they could all be in jail. Grandpa? Really? He's no criminal. Neither are the others."

She nodded. "There must have been extenuating circumstances. Maybe there was a crime, and the police misunderstood what happened, so they arrested everyone. It'll get sorted out."

"Maybe you're right." He didn't sound convinced. "I hope so."

"You're going to have to trust the Lord with this." It felt odd for her to be saying that to a pastor, but she knew Austin would take it well.

He gave her a wry, strained smile. "I know."

They joined the back of the line for Tom's Taxi. The golf cart seated four, with little room for luggage. It appeared that Tom was beginning his second trip up the island.

She glanced at Austin. "Looks like a long wait."

"Yeah." He eyed her. "Want to walk?"

Sierra shrugged. "Might as well. We might get there sooner that way."

She wasn't in any hurry, but she wasn't excited about pulling weeds for Tom, either.

They left the line and started the long walk up to the farm, hand in hand. Both were silent for a while, and Austin adjusted his grip to entwine his fingers with hers.

She didn't hide the smile it brought to her face.

As NIGHT FELL, a light rain began to sprinkle in Tel Aviv. Wu Ying turned to Lieutenant Colonel Meir, who stood beside him on the lawn of the military facility. The man finished a phone call, then pulled a tiny flashlight from his pocket and glanced at Wu Ying.

"My team will be working in portable facilities tonight. We have one trailer that is set up as a canteen. You can wait there until things get sorted out."

"Thank you." Wu Ying fell in step with the tall colonel. "I have tried to phone my friends in the city, but cannot get through to them. Are you using a dedicated service?"

"Of course. The civilian cell towers are overloaded, but we have military towers as well as satellite phones." He eyed Wu Ying. "We issued you a sat phone. Where is it?"

"In the rubble of your building, with my other belongings. I was in the cafeteria when the first quake struck, and did not have time to return to my quarters for my possessions." He glanced down at the Bible under his arm. "I am very glad to have my Bible. And I have some photos of family members, because I had placed them inside the back cover."

They started across a wide parking lot, and Colonel Meir

adjusted the beam of his flashlight to a wider area so they could avoid fallen obstacles and broken glass.

"I'm surprised you brought family photos with you to the base," Meir said.

"War was coming," Wu Ying explained. "I knew I might never return to my apartment. I brought other valuables as well, and also my passport."

"Are they also under the rubble?"

"Yes. All I have now is what was in my pockets when I went to dinner, and my Bible."

Wu Ying did not mention that he'd lost his wife's remaining jewelry and gold coins. Strangely, he was so happy to still have his Bible and the family photos, he barely worried about the lost valuables.

"It will be challenging to replace your passport," Meir said. "If you will present a list of your missing items, that will be helpful if any are located during the cleanup."

They exited the end of the parking lot and approached a gravel lot surrounded by chain link fence topped by concertina wire. Inside, emergency lights illuminated numerous portable buildings.

To Wu Ying, this resembled a smaller version of the labor camps in communist countries. He hesitated to enter when Meir opened the gate with a key on his key ring.

"Are you alright?" The colonel swung his flashlight beam up, catching Wu Ying's eyes, which he immediately closed. "What is the matter?"

"It looks like a prison camp."

"This is Israel. We have no such camps." The man's voice softened slightly. "Look, our buildings are damaged or collapsed. We're doing the best we can to keep working, because the war's not going to stop and wait for us. It's not pretty, but these trailers have generators, so there's electricity and lights. They're still functional because they're on wheels. They just rode out the quakes."

"I understand." Wu Ying swallowed his fear, which he believed was irrational, and stepped through the gate. A moment later, he was amused to have that verse from the twenty-third Psalm flit into his mind –

Yea, though I walk through the valley of the shadow of death,
I will fear no evil;
For You are with me;
Your rod and Your staff, they comfort me.

At Christian's suggestion, Wu Ying had made a point to memorize a Bible verse or short passage every day. It was a delight when one of these verses came to mind in an appropriate moment.

Gravel crunched under their shoes as Colonel Meir directed him to the nearest trailer, where he mounted some steps, then opened the door and turned on the lights for Wu Ying.

"This is our canteen. Help yourself to food and drinks. There's a television, and you can make calls out on the phone. When you get tired, you can stretch out on one of the couches."

"Thank you." Wu Ying stepped inside. Refrigerators with intact glass doors boasted an assortment of packaged salads, sandwiches and desserts, plus a variety of drinks. They were jumbled on their shelves as a result of the earthquake.

At the other end of the trailer, several couches circled a television. He suspected their locations had shifted as the canteen rode out the quakes, but nothing appeared broken.

For the moment, he had the place to himself. He glanced back at his host. "This is quite nice. I appreciate your trust."

The man chuckled. "You're welcome. I'll be in the next trailer down."

Wu Ying smiled as Meir left. Both men knew he could not really get into any trouble in the canteen trailer, but if a person intended harm to the Israeli military, he could easily leave this trailer and snoop around the rest of the complex.

He noticed a small table with a land-line telephone and decided to try to reach Wei Min and Christian. Opening his Bible on the table, he dialed Christian's number from a list he kept inside the front cover. He was unlikely to remember the phone numbers of friends and acquaintances otherwise, since he rarely actually dialed any numbers anymore.

One lovely thing about smart phones was that they allowed people to become dumber.

Not surprisingly, he could not get through to Christian. Nearly everyone in Israel was likely trying to call their friends and family tonight.

He said a prayer for his friends, then settled on a couch and turned on the television to catch the latest news of the war and the natural disasters.

26

Ivan hobbled through the entry doors of the Syrian military building with Pavlov. Both doors hung off their hinges, and no staff were in sight. The men stationed here must have fled during the horrific earthquake.

Continuous flashes of lightning filled the air with the stench of brimstone, and revealed huge shards of glass on the tile floor – a result either of the earthquake or the monstrous hailstones that still pounded Damascus.

A single emergency light dimly illuminated the entry area and cast an eerie glow on Pavlov's pale and very wrinkled face. He looked like a dead man, a zombie.

Outside, the thunder roared and boomed, competing with the screaming missiles, the wails of sirens and humans, and the explosions of war.

"Let's stay near the doors," Ivan yelled into his friend's face.

Pavlov nodded, but said nothing.

Ivan probably wouldn't have been able to hear his response anyway.

Pavlov reached toward Ivan's head, and touched below his

ear. As he drew his hand back, Ivan saw blood on the man's fingers.

"You, too!" Ivan shouted, pointing at Pavlov's ears, which had blood oozing from them.

Would they be permanently deaf, or would they regain their hearing?

He had no idea.

That was a question that might be relevant tomorrow, or next week, if they survived this night – which seemed rather unlikely at the moment.

On the bright side, he and Pavlov were no longer standing in a pool of floodwater as lightning struck everything around them.

He felt the roar of thunder in his chest. It was *that* loud.

And the storm stank – oh, how it stank of burning heat and brimstone!

Ivan slicked water off his head with his hands. How had he never known that lighting smelled so bad? Perhaps it was not the actual lighting – it might be the structures or persons the bolts were hitting with a heat five times greater than the surface of the sun.

Of course the scorch would reek.

How could his troops survive such a storm?

Perhaps it was not hitting their locations with such ferocity. Storms could be local rather than widespread.

But as he recalled how bizarrely this one formed, a massive cloud arising from a blue sky – he doubted his troops were spared.

However, Israel's troops would be caught in the same storm, would they not? Their tanks would also bog down in the muddy flood, and their soldiers would be caught out in the deadly hail. The hailstones would have hammered their equipment, too, and lightning would damage both armies.

The earthquake could not have hit the Russians while sparing the Jews.

Everyone would suffer the same damage, would they not?

This thought brought Ivan little comfort. He had no confidence in the progress of his war after an evening like this.

And still, the storm wasn't letting up. The rain poured, the hail hammered, the lightning struck and the thunder roared... all forming a shocking, cacophonous backdrop to the war that raged in the skies and exploded the buildings around him.

AS HE AND Sierra finally neared the farm, Austin grew fatigued. Not only physically from the long day and the hike up the mountain, but also mentally and spiritually. What had started as a disappointment when his family didn't arrive on the boat turned into a disaster when he learned why they failed to show up.

He could barely believe that any police officer would arrest Grandpa. He was old, frail and obviously not a criminal.

Austin's cousins weren't criminals, either.

At least, not as far as he knew. It was possible that Louis had done something stupid as a paranoid schizophrenic. He may have even been violent.

But Rick and his wife would have tried to manage Louis – they wouldn't have helped him commit a crime. And Grandpa certainly wouldn't, either.

"You doing okay?" Sierra asked softly.

He shrugged, then glanced at her. "I guess. Not happy, but okay."

"Understandable."

The sound of tires on gravel indicated Tom's Taxi was

rolling up behind them. Austin guided Sierra to the edge of the road.

If his count was correct, this was the fifth trip Tom had taken up the mountain today. He must be earning a good living. His early trips had included the community elders, the mayor and most of the newcomers. Apparently, the rest of the locals were letting everyone else go first. It made sense – the farm elders would show the new arrivals to their temporary housing in the recreation hall as they arrived, and help them settle in.

As the taxi rolled past them, Austin turned to Sierra. "What was your impression of the new people?"

"I think they'll be okay, for the most part. There are two family groups, one of six and the other of five – they all seem fine."

"And the others? Four, right?"

"Yeah." She nodded. "There's a lady in her forties. Seems nice enough. Said she knows something about herbal remedies. And a guy in his fifties, he was a construction worker."

She paused, then glanced behind them before continuing.

"I'm a little more concerned about the two younger men. Both in their twenties. One has a lot of tattoos. I mean, full sleeves, both arms. The other looks clean cut but seems to have a hard edge. A little hostile, you know? He was wearing a long-sleeved t-shirt, so I don't know whether he had ink or not."

She met his gaze. "I don't want to pre-judge them, but I'd probably keep an eye on those two."

Austin nodded. "You might mention your concerns to the elders, just in case."

"Good point."

"Did they seem to know each other?"

"Yeah, they did – but it's hard to guess how long." She

tugged on her backpack straps. "They might have met on the boat, and just hit it off together."

"Or they might be members of the same gang," Austin pointed out.

Sierra nodded. "I had wondered about that."

AS THEY APPROACHED Fellowship Farm's entrance gate, Sierra considered mentioning that it seemed like both of the suspicious guys had flirted with her a little bit. They'd been subtle. In fact, she wasn't even sure it was flirting.

If it happened again, she'd probably mention that to Austin.

As it was, it might have only been her imagination. Both Grandma and Daisy had been in earshot, and neither had said a word about it.

In any event, she had made a point of letting them know that her boyfriend was the local pastor, so it was unlikely they'd make any more advances.

"Can we talk about my cousin Louis?" Austin asked.

She nodded, happy to change the topic. "Sure."

"I've been trying to figure out how to deal with him if he does eventually come here. We won't be able to get any medication for him, obviously."

"Yes, and that reminds me...." She stopped walking and turned to face him. "I came across something in a book in Grandma's library. A doctor in Oregon, I think, was working with mental patients and came to suspect that part of their problem might be linked to a digestive disorder related to gluten. She took them off bread and found improved behavior."

"Really?" He gawked at her. "I've never heard anything like that."

"Maybe it's not orthodox," she agreed, "but reading that reminded me of a synopsis in one of my textbooks – I looked it up, and there was this scientific study on the impact of carbohydrates on schizophrenics and people with bipolar disorder. It seems there may be a connection. Carbs might trigger some of their delusional episodes or hallucinations."

"Wow. Man, if that's true... it would be amazing." Austin shook his head slowly. "But why wouldn't we know about it?"

"There's a ton of money, and I mean billions, made on drugs for psychiatric patients." She met his gaze. "Who is going to get rich off telling them to try a ketogenic diet?"

His breathing shallowed and his face reddened. "I know you're right. Stuff like that happens. But it's evil, pure evil, if simple solutions to serious problems are withheld purely from greed."

"It might not be an actual solution," she hedged. "But maybe it could help some of them. And you're right about the greed."

They turned and started in the farm's driveway.

"It reminds me of what you were saying earlier this year, about Mystery Babylon," she said.

He slowed and glanced her way. "What was that?"

"You know, the part about how she deceived the whole world with her sorcery – her pharmaceuticals." Sierra frowned. "That deception was based in pure evil. Greed and power. Many drugs are actually helpful, but there's been a flood of deception to push other drugs that were very expensive and not very effective. And American drug companies didn't only push them on the United States. They pushed them on the whole world, like it says in Revelation chapter 18."

IN THE MILITARY CANTEEN TRAILER, Wu Ying settled back into the couch and flipped through the television channels until he came to one that broadcast in English. A middle-aged male anchor sat behind a news desk with a very concerned look on his face.

"...and that wraps up the news from the southern front. On the northeastern front, at the border with Syria, the situation is equally murky. Our sources on the ground are reporting that following the earthquakes, a disastrous storm dropped at least ten centimeters of rain in less than an hour, along with hailstones as large as pomegranates and grapefruit."

He paused momentarily, then rushed on.

"The earthquakes destroyed many buildings, both in Israel and the surrounding countries, while the rain caused destabilized soil to collapse. In many locations, there are reports of massive mudslides, road washouts and bridge collapses."

The reporter blinked twice, then continued reading his script.

"On the screen behind me, you can see where a section of Mount Hermon collapsed. We believe all of Israel's mountains suffered similar landslides. And this next footage shows damage to buildings in northern Israel, near the epicenter, which was approximately sixty kilometers northeast of Nazareth, in the Golan Heights."

Wu Ying stared at the images, taken in the dim twilight during the horrific storm. Whoever had filmed that video had risked his life to do so, as monstrous hail fell in the background.

The hail pummeled vehicles, smashing in their roofs, hoods and windows. A person who ventured out in that storm surely had a death wish that would be granted.

"Meanwhile," the news anchor continued, "the fighting continued after a brief pause for the earthquakes and storms. Our military sources confirmed that hundreds of thousands of Russian, Syrian, Turkish and Iranian troops flooded through the Golan Heights before the earthquake and storm hit. Similar numbers of their Libyan, Egyptian and northern African allies invaded Israel's southern border. Also among the Russian allies are troops from eastern Europe, as well as Kazakhstan and Uzbekistan."

Wu Ying shook his head.

It was as if the entire world hated Israel and hoped to destroy it forever.

"Taking a look at the center of the country," the man continued, "Israel has been fighting off a barrage of missile and rocket attacks. These have not only been directed at military targets. The enemy is also targeting civilian structures such as hospitals, power facilities and even residential buildings, in violation of international law."

The video cut to a night-time view of a city, with incoming rockets colliding with defensive missiles mid-air over apartment buildings.

"This footage was shot in Jerusalem approximately one hour ago," the news anchor reported. "Similar scenes are now witnessed in Tel Aviv and other Israeli cities."

He looked straight into the camera. "Whether or not you consider yourself to be a religious person, please pray tonight for the peace and safety of our beloved country."

Wu Ying gawked at the screen.

Had he heard that right?

Words such as those would never be spoken on television in China.

27

The horrific storm lasted for hours, and eventually Ivan collapsed of exhaustion and slept. When he woke, the storm had finally ended. The sky cleared and the stars came out as if nothing had ever happened.

Eventually, a pale light on the horizon indicated dawn would make an appearance, after all.

Ivan and Pavlov carefully stepped out of the building they'd sheltered in, and they discovered the water outside beginning to recede.

The thunder had ended, but a few explosions continued to rock Damascus.

Ivan's ears still rang from the cacophony of the violent night. He did not see any missiles overhead, so he assumed the explosions were from gas pipelines or other hazards.

Syrian medics carried dead or dying men on stretchers toward one intact building with a universal red cross symbol emblazoned above the entrance.

"We must find President Abramov," Pavlov shouted.

"No need," Ivan yelled. "He is right there!"

The president stood outside the doors of the bunker where

they'd worked the previous day. As he turned, his gaze fell on Ivan and Pavlov. He motioned them over.

"I'm going to the front," he said. "You are coming with me."

Pavlov frowned. "That is not safe, Mister President. You could be injured."

"I will be fine." He straightened his lapel. "Let's go."

"But how?" Ivan asked. "The hail destroyed the vehicles and aircraft. The earthquake no doubt took out roads and bridges."

"Helicopter! Some were stored in a hangar that survived the earthquake and attacks. Follow me." The president turned sharply on his heel, and Ivan fell in behind him, partially supporting Pavlov, who suffered a leg injury when the table pinned him to the bunker wall.

The old man really should be getting that leg checked out, rather than venturing to the war's front. But it was obvious President Abramov would not entertain any objections or delays.

They crossed a flooded parking area, then entered a small building staffed by two Syrian officers.

President Abramov used his cell phone translation app to tell them who he was, and that he wished to go to the front lines. When they realized he was the Russian president, they seemed quite agreeable.

Five minutes later, one of the men led the Russian trio to a heliport, where a pilot was performing a pre-flight check. A Syrian interpreter stood by to provide Russian/Syrian language services.

Less than ten minutes after that, they were airborne.

The pilot flew low, which seemed reckless to Ivan, but he made excellent time. He announced the moment they reached the Israel border, which was now undefended, and he made a second announcement as they approached the front line.

The helicopter slowed somewhat, and reduced elevation to give the men a better look at the situation on the ground. The sun had not yet risen, but twilight had brightened the sky and the landscape below.

The Russian troops and their allies had swarmed the mountains last night. The Israelis still held much of the valley floor.

"Set it down," President Abramov ordered. "I wish to get out."

The pilot responded, and the interpreter translated. "I would not recommend that. It is unsafe."

"Do it anyway," the president said.

He turned to Ivan and Pavlov. "We must rally the troops and inspire them. They will see we are unafraid, and they will take courage to continue the battle vigorously."

Pavlov said nothing, and Ivan swallowed his fear. This was a reckless move for certain. They could be killed.

But there was no arguing with the president. It was obvious his mind was made up.

The pilot lowered the bird toward a wide highway and muttered something. "He says to be quick," the interpreter said.

The president did not respond to them. As soon as the chopper landed and it was safe to disembark, he did so, with Pavlov limping behind him.

With great trepidation, Ivan followed.

He did not wish to die here.

Not like this, after surviving a night of deadly horrors.

He wished to live and go home to his family.

As soon as they were out of the wind chop of the helicopter's blades, President Abramov glanced at Ivan.

"After the lightning and hailstorm, I had the cavalry sent in." He motioned to the muddy terrain. "The horses can negotiate this mucky terrain, which bogs down the tanks and personnel transports."

He grinned weirdly, and his eyes looked wild. "Plus, the horses are quiet! They made great forward progress during the night, as you will see."

Months ago, when President Abramov had decided to bring back a mounted cavalry, Ivan had strong reservations about it, but he'd kept his doubts to himself. India had only recently disbanded its cavalry. Perhaps the old methods of war could still be useful in the modern era. It remained to be seen.

In any event, Russia's modern equipment and aircraft were mostly immobile or destroyed, so advances on foot or hoof were the only ones that would happen today.

"How did the horses survive the hailstones?" Ivan looked to the president.

"Some were killed," he admitted, "but the beasts naturally seek out shelter, which they found under trees and overpasses. Many survived in a railroad tunnel."

"It is amazing that tunnel wasn't destroyed by the earthquake," Pavlov growled. "Almost everything else was."

The war's front was eerily quiet.

A few gunshots broke out, but the only significant sound was that of the helicopter.

President Abramov strode toward a group of men who had taken refuge behind a mud-swamped tank, and Ivan and Pavlov followed.

Suddenly, one of the soldiers appeared to recognize the president. He snapped to attention and saluted.

It was a foolish thing to do.

A moment later, a gunshot rang out, followed by many more.

Ivan watched, horrified, as the president's knees buckled. In slow motion, he fell face-forward into the mud.

Ivan lurched toward him. He grabbed the president's left arm and hauled him toward the tank.

Pain stabbed his back, then his chest. He lost his grip on the president, only meters from the supposed safety of the tank.

He cried out as several soldiers rushed toward them and yanked him and the president up against the hard metal of the tank's tracks.

A quick glance down confirmed the worst – red bloomed and stained the front of his uniform. The president wasn't looking good, either. He appeared to be unconscious, or possibly dead. A massive gash cut across his cheek and above his ear, and blood oozed through his clothing.

Pavlov had fallen in the mud a dozen meters away. He did not move, and no one risked their neck to attempt to retrieve him.

Ivan struggled to breathe, but could not seem to get any air. Cold seeped through his body.

He stared blankly at the sky, where a brilliant sunrise rose over the Golan Heights. Turning his eyes, he caught sight of the sparkling blue waters of the Sea of Galilee.

Slowly, his vision tunneled into darkness.

AT TEN MINUTES TO SEVEN, Austin hurried to the radio shack. If his cousins had been released from jail, they might try to make contact. Hopefully, they'd all be released by now.

He had to believe their detention was a big mistake or misunderstanding. There was no way so many members of his family had been involved in a violent crime.

No way.

As he passed the chapel, he heard footsteps behind him. He glanced back and saw Sierra.

She jogged to catch up. "I thought you might be going to the coms building."

"Absolutely." He took her hand, and they walked quickly. "I have to be there, seven o'clock, morning and evening, until I find out what happened."

"I'm sure they'll check in as soon as they can," she said.

When they reached the entrance, he held the door open for her, then followed her inside.

Alfred was powering up his equipment.

He glanced their way. "Figured you'd be coming in. Heard your family wasn't on the transport."

News traveled at gossip speed around the tiny community.

Austin settled into the chair beside him. "Yeah. I expect they'll reach out when they can."

"'Course they will." Alfred pulled on his headset. He fiddled with some knobs and dials. His gear looked like it had been new in 1980 or so.

Sierra eased onto the stool in the corner. She offered a reassuring smile, but said nothing as the clock ticked toward seven.

Suddenly, Alfred straightened, spoke a few words into the microphone, and turned to Austin. He removed his headset and pulled the cord from its jack.

"Your cousin is on."

Austin leaned toward the mic. "Rick? What happened?"

"Crazy stuff, man. Crazy stuff!" He sounded rattled. "Louis got a little weird, and went after a local guy, and it turned into a brawl outside a bar. He came running back to where we were staying, and pretty soon the cops showed up to arrest him. I tried to explain that he was mental, then Grandpa grabbed his arm to keep him here, and things got out of control and we got arrested for obstructing."

"But you're out now, obviously." Austin assumed Rick wasn't using a radio in the local jail.

"All except Louis."

"He's still in jail?"

"He's detained for a mental exam," Rick explained. "We told them he's schizophrenic, but they want to test him anyway."

"Then what?"

"Then they'll probably take him to a bigger city, and keep him in a psych facility for a while." Rick released a heavy sigh.

"What about the rest of you? Did they drop the charges?"

"Not yet, but I think they will. I don't think they want to waste legal resources on petty stuff like charging Grandpa for interfering with the arrest of a mental patient."

"I should hope not." Austin's relief at the release of most of his family was tempered by his concern for their legal situation. Not to mention housing. "So what now? Do you have a place to stay?"

"Yeah. A local church opened its doors, so we're staying there. It's across the street from a grocery store, and there's a truck stop with showers about two blocks away."

"How's Grandpa?"

"He's fine. A little confused about all this, but happy to be out of jail and back with me and Sheri."

"Good. Good." Austin exhaled a breath. "And you and Sheri? How are you guys?"

"Hanging in there. Hating life lately, but we're okay, all things considered."

"If there's anything I can do –"

"Thanks. Pray for us. Oh, did you hear the big news?"

"About the war in Israel?"

Rick chuckled. "No, I meant here, in Canada. Apparently there's been some international outrage about the expulsion of American refugees, and Canadian officials have relented on kicking us all out of their country. So for now, we can stay. After jumping through some bureaucratic hoops, of course."

"That's great! Really. Canada is so much better off than we are." Austin glanced toward Sierra, who grinned and gave him two thumbs up.

SIERRA FELT ALMOST GIDDY to learn that Canada would not be deporting all the U.S. refugees. Hopefully, that would mean there would not be any more transports dumping strangers off at Hideaway's dock.

Compared to the United States, Canada still had a functional nation. Their west coast was decimated by the megatsunami, of course, and they were getting wind-blown radiation from the United States, but they still had a power grid that worked, and farmers harvesting their food, and gas and oil and grocery deliveries to the majority of their population.

It wouldn't hurt them all that much to absorb a million Americans.

She listened as Austin wrapped up his radio conversation.

After he signed off, he turned to her.

For the first time today, he appeared genuinely happy. "What a relief! Praise the Lord!"

She smiled and slid off her stool. "Amen."

Alfred eyed them. "Glad that worked out okay. And really glad Canada's gonna stop evicting all the Americans."

Austin turned to him. "Thanks, Alfred. I really appreciate your help with all this."

"No problem." He gave a nod. "By the way, have you had a chance to follow the news in Israel today?"

"Not really," Austin admitted.

Sierra looked to the ham operator. "What's the latest?"

As he filled them in on what he'd heard, she shook her head in amazement.

"Wow. That's just... amazing."

"You can say that again," Alfred said. "I've been glued to the news. Could hardly believe it myself."

Austin nodded.

"It's astonishing, right? And yet, it was revealed to Ezekiel so long ago." He paused momentarily. "Oh! That reminds me of a verse... where is it? I'll have to look it up, but it says the Lord does nothing without first revealing His secrets to His servants the prophets."

Sierra grinned. "I read that last week. It's in Amos. Chapter three, I think."

"That's it." Austin snapped his fingers. "Chapter three, verse seven."

She tilted her head. "I wonder why? Why does He reveal things ahead of time?"

"Lots of reasons, I suspect." He smiled at her. "It brings glory to His name. It brings understanding and peace to His people – they know some of what's going to happen, and how it will work out in the end. It builds up their faith. Perhaps it draws skeptics to the Lord, as well."

Alfred turned off his radio gear. "I'd think it'd be pretty convincing that God is real, when His prophets announce something years or millennia in advance, and then the world watches it happen in real time."

"And yet, many will refuse to believe," Austin pointed out. "The Bible says people believe lies because they hate the truth."

Sierra frowned. "That's so sad."

He reached for her hand. "It is. But everyone gets to make their own choice. The Lord doesn't force anyone to believe in Him. He gives us all free will."

ALTHOUGH HE WAS hungry and thirsty, Wu Ying could not tear himself away from the television in the canteen trailer. Every minute brought astonishing new revelations. Every channel carried only news of the war and natural disasters, and rarely did they break for commercials.

He watched as a man transfixed.

An English-speaking woman had taken the place of the male newscaster he had previously been watching. She was younger, perhaps late twenties, with glossy auburn hair and intriguing hazel eyes. Her lips were done in a garish hue, which unfortunately highlighted the fact that they were not symmetrical.

Wu Ying tried to ignore this, but found it oddly distracting.

Astonishment registered in her face as she read her teleprompter. "We have verified reports of invading troops firing upon each other in the Golan Heights and mountains of Israel. Not only that, but similar reports are coming in now from the southern front."

She gulped. "At this time, we are unable to confirm a reason for this infighting. Are the Russian allies turning upon each other intentionally? Were they confused by communications issues arising from hail damage or language difficulties? Our sources are looking into that, but so far do not have a firm explanation.

"We have confirmed that their death toll is rising exponentially. They are killing each other, and at the same time, the

Israel Defense Forces are pressing their attack. The total numbers of dead are unconfirmed, but our military sources report it is in the hundreds of thousands. That is the invading allies only. Israel is believed to have lost about ten thousand soldiers."

She inhaled a huge breath before continuing.

"Here in Jerusalem, the fighting rages in the air, and now on the streets as terrorists take advantage of the war situation to attack Jewish institutions and homes. Martial law was imposed twelve hours ago, with curfews for all civilians, but there is some lack of enforcement of those rules as the military is more focused on repelling military attacks such as missiles and bombs, rather than civilian ones on the ground."

She paused and pressed a finger to her earpiece. Her face blanched as she focused again on the camera.

"We are getting news at this moment that something has happened on Temple Mount. We are attempting to get verification and video feed, but there has been some sort of attack."

She moistened her lips.

The video behind her switched to a view of the Dome of the Rock.

Wu Ying stared. He squinted at the television.

Was he seeing that right?

It looked like... like the golden Islamic shrine had been obliterated.

"As you can see behind me..." the reporter stared in astonishment. "As you can see... it appears that the Dome of the Rock and Al-Aqsa Mosque have suffered serious damage."

Serious damage?

Wu Ying stood up and approached the television.

That was far more than serious damage!

From his military background and experience, he was certain the shrine had been hit with multiple missiles.

The newscaster eventually found her voice and continued her report, but Wu Ying focused on the images in shock.

If such a thing had transpired at an earlier point in history, it would surely have caused a massive war in the Middle East between the Muslims and the Jews.

But now, the Jews' enemies were already at war with Israel. It was too late to go to war over this. They were already at war, and now their shrine was collateral damage.

He blinked and focused on the images.

The Dome of the Rock did not appear to be repairable. It could perhaps be rebuilt... but would the Jews allow that, if they won this war? Why should they, if they triumphed now? It would only reward their enemies for attacking them.

No, he could not imagine a situation in which Israel, if it survived this war, would ever allow the Muslim shrine to be rebuilt on Temple Mount.

The Muslims would be done here, and the Jews would finally have control of their historic temple site.

What would they do with it?

EPILOGUE

Wu Ying remained at the military facility for two more days while the war died out as Russia's allies killed each other. He watched, along with the whole world, as Israel triumphed over her enemies.

Finally, he was able to make phone contact with Christian and Wei Min, and learned that their apartment building remained standing. Wei Min had also ventured out to Wu Ying's apartment to see if he had returned, and reported that his building had suffered a total collapse from the earthquake.

Wu Ying sent up a prayer of thanks for his providential move to the military facility before the war began.

He felt blessed to have a couch to sleep on in the canteen trailer, but at the first opportunity, he volunteered to join a civilian crew searching through wreckage for surviving victims of the quakes and war.

It was dusty, sad work, but there were moments of rejoicing, such as the moment he helped pull a five-year-old boy out from under a fallen wall, followed by his uninjured three-year-old sister. Their mother wept tears of relief all over their dirt-stained faces.

At the end of each long day, he turned on the television to see if any more astonishing news had transpired.

On the second evening, a journalist interviewed Israel Defense Forces in the Golan Heights. The triumphant men and women had gathered around a campfire. But there was something peculiar about the wood in the fire.

Wu Ying peered at the television screen and blinked.

Were those... guns?

Maybe his tired mind was playing tricks on him, but it looked as if the IDF was burning rifles in their campfire!

He shook his head, blinked, and looked again.

Finally, the female reporter seemed to notice the oddity. She asked about them it.

Wu Ying read the chyron transcript as it scrolled across the bottom of the screen.

"Soldiers are celebrating their victory with festive meals cooked over campfires. As you can see here, they are burning rifles. When we asked about this, our soldiers said the Russians carried a mix of modern weaponry and older rifles with wooden stocks. These, we are told, are Mosin-Nagant rifles, of which over 35 million were produced. The soviets, followed by the Russians, had stockpiled millions of these weapons."

The reporter faced the camera directly and continued. "Local residents have been rushing out and collecting these relics, along with other weaponry and items of value. The military discourages this behavior, stating it is unsafe and potentially dangerous."

After the on-site journalist wrapped up her report, the woman running the anchor desk began a story on the destruction of the Dome of the Rock.

"Civilians have also been scavenging gold and artifacts at the Dome of the Rock and the Al-Aqsa Mosque, which were both destroyed during the war. This theft is illegal, but police have been unable to contain the celebratory crowds that have rushed to Temple Mount as the war ended. Now, numerous Jewish groups and leaders are advocating for a rebuilding of the Jewish Temple."

The anchor woman showed little emotion as she continued reading her script. "Of course, some of these religious groups have spent years amassing the necessary funds and supplies for such a project, which they see as a necessary component prior to the arrival of the Messiah.

"For details, we turn to Rabbi Asher Rabin. Rabbi, what is your take on the situation at the Temple Mount?"

An ultra-orthodox rabbi looked gravely into the camera. "It is time to rebuild the temple. We must begin immediately. Establish the temple on its rightful, historic location, and prepare for the Messiah."

The anchor woman looked concerned. "But surely that will infuriate Muslims everywhere."

"Does it matter now? Our enemies have attempted, once again, to annihilate the Jews, and they have again failed. They did not only attempt to conquer our country, but it was obvious they intended to murder all of us."

He tilted his head. "By whatever means, whether the enemy's missiles or an act of God, the dome and the mosque have been obliterated. The people themselves are sweeping the site clean. Now we must move forward and rebuild the temple."

After a few more words, the news station cut to a commercial, and Wu Ying muted the television.

This was amazing. He shook his head at the astonishing turn of events.

He would only imagine what might happen next, but he

was happy to be here, in Israel, to witness this amazing time in history.

And more than that, he was glad to have Jesus in his heart, and be able to walk in His footsteps here in the Holy Land, where the swift gazelle had once again escaped the predators who tried so hard to destroy her.

The End.

～

Thank you for reading this series.
My newsletter readers will be notified when my next novel is ready.
You can sign up at www.JamieLeeGrey.com.

LETTER TO READERS

Dear friends,

Thank you for choosing this series. I hope you enjoyed it. Would you do me a favor and write a quick review on the site where you bought it? It will help me as an author, and it will help your fellow readers decide whether this book is for them. **Thank you very much!**

If you'd like to communicate with me, you can contact me at my website, www.JamieLeeGrey.com

May God's face shine upon you and bring you peace.

All the best,

Jamie Lee Grey

ACKNOWLEDGMENTS

I am indebted to independent military analysts and geopolitical analysts who have long been sounding the alarm about Russia and China, and the Marxist/communist threat in general. Their research and opinions have shaped my own.

We all owe a huge debt of gratitude to the many dissidents of tyrannical nations who have risked their lives to escape and to warn the rest of the world of the great calamity that is coming upon us.

Special thanks to John Rock and Deb Motley for their feedback, prayers and encouragement.

Candle Sutton – For over a decade, Candle has been my amazing critique partner, a true friend and partner in prayer. (Check out Candle's books at www.CandleSutton.com .)

My husband – You are the best. Thank you for your encouragement and support. I love you.

Jesus Christ – My life and breath, my inspiration and the giver of all good gifts. Thank You.

ALSO BY JAMIE LEE GREY

Book 4: The Lion

Book 5: The Gazelle

Stand-alone novel:

Holy War

～

My newsletter readers will be notified when my next novel is ready.

Sign up at www.JamieLeeGrey.com

God bless you and keep you!